HEAVEN
IN
HIGH GEAR

Also by Joan Brady

God on a Harley

HEAVEN
IN
HIGH GEAR

JOAN BRADY

POCKET BOOKS
New York   London   Toronto   Sydney   Tokyo   Singapore

POCKET BOOKS, a division of Simon & Schuster Inc.
1230 Avenue of the Americas, New York, NY 10020

ISBN: 0-671-00772-6

First Pocket Books hardcover printing August 1997

10 9 8 7 6 5 4 3 2 1

For Laura, my sister. She knows why.

Acknowledgments

Any writer who is fortunate enough to have a book published probably did not do it without the help of some very important people. In my case, there have been many. I have been blessed to have each and every one of them in my life, and this is where I publicly thank them.

My parents, Thomas and Claire Brady, encouraged me and nurtured the seeds of my blossoming ability to write for as long as I can remember. My sisters, Patricia and Laura, and my brothers, Paul, Tom, Bo, and Ed, believed in me from the start and never once wavered in their confidence that I would succeed. And always, I shared my dreams with Nancy, my friend since childhood.

My agent, Denise Stinson, has once again worked her magic by giving me exactly enough input to bring out the best in me. I am also blessed to have for my editor Emily Bestler, who expertly takes my work to new heights.

Several of my fellow writers have helped in a myriad of ways. Teresa Allen shot the wonderful photographs for both of my book jackets and is a supportive and insightful presence in my life. Joan Swirsky gave me a loving and generous headstart on the road to literary success. Chris Hall escorted me to the places where I did my research and made me feel safe. Vista Publishing, Inc., of Long Branch, New Jersey, deserves a round of applause for giving first-time authors a chance to show the world what they've got.

Finally, I will always remember my dear friend, Patrick, for helping me to find my wings . . . and for teaching me to soar.

I am deeply grateful to all of you.

HEAVEN
IN
HIGH GEAR

1

IN SPITE OF THE FACT THAT I was back in New Jersey, I had two things going for me: it was summer and I was down at the shore. If you absolutely *have* to be in Jersey for any reason whatsoever, it's always a good idea to avoid those brutal winter months. You definitely don't want to be cooped up with a bunch of people who haven't seen the sun for five straight months and who are all suffering from Seasonal Affective Disorder. Of course they're all in a state of denial about their condition and won't admit to it. I should know. I grew up there and I used to be one of them.

I had just flown in from LA the night before (or "La-La Land," as they like to call it here) for my biannual visit to the old home front. It's a ritual I endure in order to keep *them* from flying out to visit *me*. The way I see it, my life is my own and nobody from my "growing up years" needs to know that I make my living as a stripper.

In contrast to my sixteen peers who work alongside me at the Pink Pussycat in LA, I'm the only one who doesn't try to sugarcoat the facts by calling herself an "exotic dancer" or a "performer." Whom do they think they're kidding? Taking off your clothes, even if you dance around while doing it, is still stripping in my book. Unlike the rest of them, I'm not the least bit ashamed of what I do. If I don't strip, I don't eat. For that matter, if I didn't strip, I wouldn't be driving my coveted BMW or living in Brentwood either. It's as simple as that. Besides, I don't see anybody else paying the mortgage on my condo or making my car payments, so whatever I do to survive is *my* business, right?

Of course, if you saw me when I had my clothes *on,* you would have quite a different opinion of me. The way I see it, I don't get to wear clothes often enough, so when I do, I wear only the best. I know good things, and I don't hesitate to buy them for myself.

I must admit, I'm the only one of the bunch who looks like she was born with a silver spoon in her *mouth* instead of in her nose. Drugs, that's one thing I never got into, and that's what separates me from all those losers who work and hang out at the Pink Pussycat. I work too hard for this perfect body to ever consider handing it over to the demon of drugs. No, sir. Instead, I prefer to spend my money adorning it with Chanel suits, eighteen-karat-gold jewelry, and Ferragamo shoes.

Speaking of Ferragamo shoes, I looked down at the one I was dangling a bit seductively from my perfectly pedicured foot as I waited at the bar for my ever-tardy friends. I

3

suppose you can take the girl out of the strip joint, but you can't necessarily take the strip joint out of the girl. I slipped the shoe back on my foot in spite of the admiring glances I was getting from three guys at a nearby table. I had to clean up my act and remember that I was back in my hometown now. Temporarily, thank God.

It was a little past midnight here on the East Coast, but my body clock said it was only nine, so I wasn't even close to peaking yet. Three of my girlfriends were supposed to meet me here in this beachfront dive for a little "welcome home" get together, but as usual, they were extremely late. That left me only one choice: to sit alone at the bar, sipping my white wine and thinking about my life and how it measured up against the lives of my cronies.

To begin with, we are an unlikely group of friends. We have very distinct personalities and interests, and we all grew up in different towns. About the only thing we have in common is that we all spent glorious childhood summers at the Jersey shore with our families, and that is the glue that holds us together.

Maria and Barbara are "Bennies," which of course means they live north of exit 117 on the Garden State Parkway. Crystal is a "Shoebee" from Philadelphia. I think they call them that because, for some unknown reason, people from Philadelphia never seem to take their shoes off, even when they're on the beach. You always see them walking through the sand with their milk-white legs and old beat-up shoes. I am the only "Clamdigger" in the group, so called because I live several exits south of 117 on the parkway near Asbury Park, which makes me the only one who lived at the shore year-round when we were all growing up.

Now, in case you haven't noticed, I'm not exactly the most politically correct person you'll ever meet, but at least I say what's on my mind. I've been accused of a lot of things in my life, but mincing words isn't one of them.

So there I was, hanging out in this somewhat "hip" little dive, waiting for my friends to show up so we could all tell each other how good we look and make up stories about how successful our careers are and how we all have boyfriends or fiancés who adore us. I'd heard that both Maria and Crystal had just become engaged to their boyfriends. I knew because my mother sent me the clippings from the newspaper announcing the joyous news. Why do mothers always send their hopelessly single daughters newspaper clippings of other people's engagements? Do they really think we want to read that stuff? Not that I couldn't be married if I wanted to be. That's hardly the case. It's just that, from what I've seen, who needs the headache?

The worst part, of course, was that I would now have to run out and buy some very expensive bridal shower and wedding gifts. After all, I had a classy image to maintain, and buying the costliest gifts and presenting them with a gracious smile would only enhance my already enviable social status in these parts.

Nonetheless, bridal showers are one ritual I never thought made much sense. I mean, why is it that when your girlfriend finally finds someone to support her or at least to help her pay the bills, all her single girlfriends who are struggling to survive on their own have to run out and buy her presents? I can't tell you how many irons and blenders I've grudgingly bought for people who could finally afford their own. The world's a very cruel place for us single people. At least these days I could afford it, but is it any wonder that I took off for the West Coast years ago to make a better life for myself?

Well, at least my life *sounded* a whole lot more exciting than Maria's and Crystal's mundane existence of beer-drinking construction-worker boyfriends who would turn into beer-drinking construction-worker husbands. For years now I've had them all convinced that I work as a makeup artist on the movie sets of Hollywood. I always enjoy the envy in their eyes as I embellish my LA lifestyle and make it all sound exciting and glamorous. I have a real flair for storytelling, and I knew I could paint a fabulous and enticing picture of life in Tinsel Town. The best part is that I never have to prove my story, since I live three thousand miles away, so they simply have to take my word for how glorious a life I live. Besides, the truth might only disappoint them.

Fortunately, I really look the part of the "oh-so-cool" California hard body. I'm tall, five feet ten, to be exact, and the California lifestyle of healthy eating and constant exercise has made me much thinner and more muscular than I used to be. This "buffed" look apparently creates an optical illusion of increased height, and you won't hear me complaining about that. Tall women seem to intimidate men, and I often find great pleasure in that, especially when I'm onstage at the club.

Speaking of clubs, where the heck were my girlfriends? They were at least half an hour late, not that this was unusual for them. I took a sip of my white wine and looked up at the still empty stage, searching for signs of this Jim MaGuire character, the musician who was featured here tonight. Wherever he was, he'd better be good because I had just paid a ten-dollar cover charge to hear him and I expected him to earn his keep. I was feeling surprisingly relaxed and maybe even a bit like dancing if he turned out to be any good. Call it a busman's holiday, but I really do like to dance.

I scanned the room one more time for my friends and came up empty, though I couldn't help but notice an odd little scenario taking place down the bar.

There was a guy and girl leaning against the bar, engrossed in a seemingly very heavy conversation. The girl looked to be in her early to mid thirties and was dressed in jeans, a white T-shirt, and white high-top sneakers. Immediately, I knew she was a nurse. Don't ask me how I know things like that, I just do. Reading people is just one of my many talents. Besides, she had that aura that nurses seem to have, you know, obviously more concerned with other people than she was about her own appearance. Give me twenty minutes with her, the right clothes and makeup, and I could probably make her into a knockout. But she wasn't the one who intrigued me. He was.

He wasn't suave enough to be a New Yorker, but he was no Clamdigger or Shoe-bee either. Whatever he was, he was saying something that made the girl cry. I watched him tenderly wipe a tear from her face (that's when I was *certain* he wasn't a New Yorker) and then anchor a strand of honey-colored hair behind her ear. She said something to him then, and he smiled and kissed the tip of her nose. There was incredible affection between them, and it was apparent that they shared some very special bond.

At that moment, a feeling of almost unbearable loneliness swept over me. Whatever their relationship was, a lot of love and tenderness was woven through it, and suddenly I ached for the lack of it in my own life. That kind of sentimental yearning is completely out of character for me, and I was a little unnerved by it. It didn't keep me from feeling sorry for myself though. For some reason I started thinking about what would happen if I died in a plane crash on the way back to LA. Who would identify my body? Probably the only one who could would be Peter, my manicurist,

who would know me by the "French pedi-
cures" he's been giving me lately. How sad is
that?

I was grateful the lights went down at that
moment, engulfing the room in darkness and
mercifully blinding me to the loving scene I
had just witnessed. I turned my full attention
to the stage instead and to the sinewy, graceful form of Jim MaGuire. I must admit, I was
immediately mesmerized by his music. Fragile strains of it drifted through me, delicately
penetrating some long-forgotten place in my
heart, and I marveled that anyone could coax
such absolute magic and beauty out of a
saxophone. Wasn't I the sensitive one tonight?

I put my empty glass on the bar and stood
with my eyes closed, drinking in the magnificence of the moment. I didn't even care if
anyone saw me in such an entranced state. It
was worth it.

Someone did.

Without even opening my eyes, I knew he
was standing beside me, and I also knew that
he was smiling. It occurred to me that this
clairvoyant thing was a little spooky, yet I

didn't feel capable of fear in his company. He just had a kind of presence that seemed to transcend closed eyelids, and what was so scary about that? As long as he stayed quiet and didn't interrupt this blissful moment, I really didn't care what he did. But wait a minute, maybe I should be scared. After all, how did I know that someone had just walked up beside me if my eyes were closed? And how did I know it was the same guy who had just kissed that girl on the tip of her nose? I don't know. Maybe it was that incredible talent or sixth sense of mine. I'm always sensing all kinds of things that other people never seem to notice. What I didn't understand was, what kind of guy makes his girlfriend cry and then saunters off and stands next to someone else?

I stood there ignoring him, totally immersing myself in the music. Every once in a while I stole a peek at him from the corner of my eye, and every time I did, he was staring back at me. What was with this guy? Not that I'm surprised when men stare at me, but you'd think he could have been a little more subtle about it. I figured he had to be some kind of wacko or something, and I should know. I tend to attract that type. I don't know what it is about me, but put me in a room with a hundred people and if there is one nut among them, he will make a beeline for me. It's not just because of the way I look either, although being a tall, lanky blonde with a fondness for spandex doesn't exactly make me inconspicuous. Something more mysterious than that attracts them.

I think it's an energy or some weird vibration they must pick up from me. I know for a fact it's not my kind and sensitive heart, because I don't have one. I learned long ago that feeling sorry for someone, especially if it's a man, is the beginning of my own demise. So this guy could just forget it. He'd find no warm and sympathetic heart here.

I had a major insight into this phenomenon one night when I was watching *America's Most Wanted.* I watch that show faithfully every Saturday night with the phone right beside me. I study the perpetrators' pictures very carefully, ready to spot any of my old boyfriends so I can dime them out. Sooner or later, I just know, one of them is bound to show up there. Anyway, this one night I was watching the show and the police were using dogs to help them hunt for a missing person. They gave the dogs a sniff of her blouse and then followed as the frantic hounds went into some kind of hunting frenzy, leading police to the exact spot where the victim was buried in a shallow grave. Then it all made sense to me. That's why nuts are always attracted to me. They must pick up some kind of special scent like those hunting dogs and know exactly where to go.

14

I sneaked another glance at the man standing beside me, and I had to admit, he looked harmless enough, but then, don't they always? He seemed lost in the music now, so I figured it was safe to study him while he wasn't looking.

His body wasn't bad as men's bodies go, but it showed no sign of long hours at the gym working out to impress the likes of me. I like men to have extremely muscular arms and shoulders. It shows they care. It shows they've really worked at their bodies. The way I see it, with their natural abundance of muscle mass and bountiful supply of testosterone, men don't have to work half as hard for a great body as we women do. I slave to keep my body in great shape, and I expect them to do the same. A fat, out-of-shape man is much more inexcusable than a fat, out-of-shape woman.

Don't get me wrong, now. It's not that this guy was fat or out of shape, not by a long shot. It's just that he obviously wasn't concerned about sculpting his body into a work of art, and being the enlightened person that I am, that was a major turnoff. My old boyfriends may all show up on *America's Most Wanted* sooner or later, but believe you me, they'll look damn good on television.

He must have been more than six feet tall, because I was wearing heels and he was still taller than me. I looked down to see if he was wearing those boots with a stacked heel that you usually see short men wear, you know, so they can trick women into thinking they're taller than they really are. Not a chance. This guy was wearing sneakers. Spotless white Nikes.

Next, I studied his clothes because a woman can tell a lot about a man by the clothes he wears. His jeans were just the right combination of used enough to be cool, but not so well worn as to look like he needed to blow himself to a new pair. I kind of liked that.

His belly was nice and flat, and I couldn't help noticing the belt that slinked around his trim waist. I couldn't be sure, but it looked like genuine snakeskin. Was this guy a cowboy or something? In a way, I kind of hoped so. Those renegade, bad-boy types always get my attention.

Now I was up to the white T-shirt he was wearing that did nothing to hide a broad pair of shoulders and muscular chest, which had to be genetic, since I'm certain he wasn't the type to work out. Though his skin was evenly tanned, he didn't seem like the sunbathing type either, so I figured him for the outdoorsy, maybe motorcycle type.

Even though it had to be at least eighty degrees outside in spite of the midnight hour, he wore a black leather jacket with the sleeves rolled up. He didn't seem to be the least bit aware of the heat, but that sleeve thing made me wonder about his sexual preference. It was kind of a borderline thing, and most women probably wouldn't even think twice about it, but being the astute and experienced person that I am, I had to wonder. Not that it mattered at all to me. I wasn't the least bit interested in a relationship with this guy. I was just curious.

Last, but certainly not least, was his face. Now, normally, that's the first thing I look at (after I make sure they have a perfect body) because faces, to me, are fascinating. He had a rather large head, but it was nicely shaped and seemed to "go" with the rest of him. His hair was dark and thick and cut perfectly to flatter his masculine features. Obviously the man had confidence, because his hair was styled back from his face, revealing a slightly receding hairline and emphasizing a nose that, though prominent, matched the rest of his features in an appealingly masculine way. His hair was conservatively short in the front, then fell into a rather long and roguish look in the back. His eyebrows were dark and thick, and they shaded smoldering brown eyes that lured me to fall into them. His cheekbones were high (I was jealous) and the side of his face curved down to a mouth that was almost pretty. There was a hint of a heavy beard peeking through his olive complexion, and it added a sense of masculine balance to his flawless skin. I've always wondered how men get that rugged, five o'clock shadow without going over the fine line of actually growing a beard. They must know exactly how many hours in advance to shave to give them just the right look by midnight. However they do it, this guy had it down to a science.

The music ended and the ceiling lights went on again, causing most of us to squint as our eyes adjusted to the sudden brightness. I learned long ago that bright, unshaded lights are the enemy of any woman over the age of twenty-five, and I was already four years beyond the cutoff point. Not that I'm especially vain or anything; it's just that in my business, a woman's youth and good looks are essential to making a good living. I was trying to avoid squinting because everybody knows it contributes to the development of those dreaded crow's feet around the eyes, and I certainly can't afford that. I noticed, though, that he never seemed to blink or to squint. He just stood there with this kind of calm and steady gaze. It was most peculiar.

Even more peculiar than that, I was finding myself immensely attracted to him.

At least, that's what I thought it was at first. You know, the fluttering heart, the sudden bolt of tension that shoots through you, and that sensation of feeling choked up. Then with absolute horror, I realized those were not the symptoms of attraction, but rather the advent of one of my god-awful, unpredictable panic attacks.

Oh, God, no. Please not here. Not now. But I knew better than to expect an anxiety attack to listen to reason.

The room began closing in on me, and my heart raced faster than one of those bloodhounds who'd just got a whiff of the victim's clothing. It became difficult to catch my breath and my throat began to close. I was paralyzed with fear and could think of nothing else but gasping for my next breath and fleeing from that room.

I knew I had only a minute, maybe just seconds, to reach into my purse for the Xanax that sometimes helps abort these attacks. I had to take it quickly though, or I would not even be capable of placing it under my tongue.

Hands trembling almost violently, I somehow managed to find the little bottle in the bottom of my purse and shake one of the orange pills out into the palm of my hand.

The first one slid uncontrollably between my shaking fingers and nose-dived to the floor. More panicked than ever now, I desperately tried to shake another one out, but this time all twenty-four remaining pills sailed through my quivering fingers and scattered hopelessly in all directions.

I spotted one that landed next to my shoe and somehow managed to scoop it up. I stood up and tried to get it to my mouth, but just as it was only millimeters from my eager lips, a large, warm hand settled on my wrist, then closed gently over my fingers.

"Don't," said a kind, soft voice close to my ear. "I know a better way."

I looked up to see that the man I'd just been studying and judging so intently was smiling down at me with enormous sympathy in his eyes. "Your panic is your friend," he continued gently. "It loves you and it's just trying to protect you."

I couldn't answer because I was still immobilized by anxiety, but apparently he wasn't expecting a reply. He simply continued to calm me in a low, soothing voice as he placed his other hand ever so gently on the side of my face.

"Don't try to fight it," he said comfortingly. "Terror isn't the enemy you think it is. Your body loves you, and it would never do anything to hurt you. Embrace your fear. This is your body's way of rescuing you from something that it thinks might hurt you." He stroked the side of my face with a touch soft as a feather.

His words had a miraculous effect on me. I'd never before thought about these panic attacks in a positive light, but when I heard this stranger telling me to love my panic and to embrace rather than resist it, I felt my heart lift its foot off the gas pedal. Within a few more seconds, my breathing became regular and easy again and I no longer felt like I was choking. My vision cleared up next, and I was able to turn to him and look into his lovely face.

I wanted to throw myself at his feet and thank him profusely for what he had done. I wanted to tell him how terrifying these attacks were, but somehow I think he already knew. I wanted to ask him a million questions, like who was he and how did he know to do that and how could I learn to do it for myself? I was overwhelmed with gratitude and curiosity, yet I was surprisingly unable to verbalize any of what I was feeling.

He pressed a long, graceful finger on the pulse of my wrist and held me rapt with his eyes. "You're all right now." He smiled. "Everything's going to be fine." Then, looking to the far corner of the room, he added, "Your friends are over there waiting for you."

I looked up and sure enough, there they were, waving wildly and making their way toward me. I was stunned that this stranger had also known who my friends were, but when I turned to confront him, he was gone.

I looked down at my wrist where he had felt my pulse, and something sparkled there. It looked like a little piece of silver glitter and I brushed it away.

Oddly, goose bumps raced up my arm.

WE STAYED TILL LAST CALL that night, laughing and drinking, catching up on gossip and embellishing our life stories. As usual, guys kept making passes at me, but I'm used to that kind of thing. I just ignored them, which of course only made them try that much harder. I don't know what it is with me, but I just don't seem to need men the way my girlfriends do. The way I see it, who needs a boyfriend as long as you have Triple A? They fix your flat tires, get you gas if you run out, and never yell at you for being stupid. If Triple A ever expands their services to taking out the garbage, they could quite possibly wipe out the institution of marriage as we know it. Besides, almost every guy who made a pass at me had a physical flaw of some kind, and as I mentioned before, I do not even consider men whose bodies are less than perfect.

Throughout the night, I found myself watching the door for that mysterious guy who had staved off my panic attack. Though he had probably hightailed it out of there on one of the many Harleys I had seen parked out front, I just couldn't get him off my mind. *No one* had ever been able to say just the right thing like that when I'm having one of my anxiety attacks. I was absolutely awestruck by the way he had talked me through it, and now my normally cold heart was filled with gratitude for his kindness. Of course I wasn't foolish enough to let my guard down completely, since he had really spooked me by knowing who my friends were. Even spookier than that was when I asked my friends if they had seen him standing next to me and they had no idea whom I was talking about. Usually they notice every guy who even glances my way, hoping to pick up my leftovers, I suppose. It struck me as very odd that they had been so completely oblivious this time, and even when I began to describe him, they just stared blankly at me. What was going on here? Who *was* that guy?

My first thought was that maybe he was a stalker and, therefore, a master of blending into a crowd, yet somehow I wasn't concerned. Whatever and whoever he was, he had just performed a miracle as far as I was concerned, and I wanted to know more about him.

I turned my attention back to the girl I'd seen him talking to earlier, the nursie-looking one who'd been crying. Now her tears had dried and she was happily chatting with Jim MaGuire, her previous companion nowhere in sight. A few minutes later, the cool musician took her hand and led her toward the door to the parking lot, where I was certain he had parked his motorcycle, most likely a Harley. It didn't take a whole lot of intuition to figure that one out, since this place tends to attract more "Hogs" than a convention of Vietnam vets. Apparently she was fully recovered now, and I was jealous that she could so easily forget the guy who just an hour ago seemed to be breaking her heart. Why was it that suddenly *I* couldn't forget him? Go figure.

My friends were at the bar getting their final drink orders in for last call, but I decided to pass. I was staying with my family in Sea Bright, a small, low-lying beach community that is famous for three things: hip bars, getting flooded during winter storms, and DUI checkpoints every Friday and Saturday night during the summer. I definitely wanted to avoid the suspicious, challenging scrutiny of the state troopers on the way home who would inevitably pull me into their red-flared lion's den.

The bare-bulbed lights came on again, making everyone squint and look worse than they do in a department store dressing-room mirror. I waited for my friends to finish their drinks while I watched one of the bouncers steer the crowd, like a shepherd guiding sheep, toward the front door. Every now and then there would be a couple of drunken strays, but the bouncer, whose body looked like a refrigerator box with a head on it, expertly rounded them up and got them out the door.

Barbara, Maria, Crystal, and I all walked out together. We stood in the parking lot for a while longer, chatting over the sounds of cars pulling out of the gravel driveway and motorcycles popping their clutches and blasting off into the night. Then we hugged each other good night and headed in different directions for our cars.

I slid into my rented Camaro and tooted the horn as I pulled out into the two AM trickle of traffic. Automatically, I opened the sunroof and breathed in the clean, smoke-free air. I know it sounds crazy, but I enjoy a sunroof more at night than I do during the day. I love looking up at the stars and the hazy summer sky and smelling the clean, ocean air.

The night was steamy and sultry, just the way I like it. In fact, these muggy East Coast nights are probably the only thing I do miss about New Jersey. LA may be touted as having perfect weather, and God knows it's a far sight better than Jersey in the winter, but the West Coast never gets quite warm enough in the summer to suit my taste.

Once safely out of earshot of my friends, I turned on the car radio to the easy-listening station. I know that's the last thing they would expect from someone as hip as me. After all, I have an image to maintain, especially living in LA and all, and I didn't want to disappoint them. I turned up the volume and belted out a duet with Whitney Houston, sounding pretty darn good if you ask me. I figured maybe when I got back to LA, I'd take singing lessons at one of those adult-education places I always see advertised. The truth was, I'd always had this secret dream of becoming a lounge singer, maybe even in Vegas. I know it's not exactly the highest aspiration in the world, but I love to sing those old, romantic, emotional songs. I swear I was born to do it.

Actually I suspect I have a real talent in that area. I've been told I have the kind of voice that kindles all sorts of intriguing images when men talk to me on the phone. It's not much of an accomplishment, I know, but more than once I've been told that I "give good phone," no matter what the topic of conversation. And I can carry a tune too.

Whitney and I were just hitting that last high note together when I saw the unmistakable red flares of the state troopers up ahead. They always set up their DUI checkpoints here because it is the only portion of Ocean Avenue that runs along a narrow strip of land between the river and the ocean, leaving nowhere to turn around inconspicuously if you've had too much to drink. You are now trapped like a rat. Of course, if you're dumb enough to drink and drive, you probably deserve to be trapped that way. To me, though, it is nothing more than a minor nuisance, since I never have more than one glass of wine in an evening.

Traffic was at a standstill while several troopers, each one more handsome than the last, walked along the row of cars, stopping to lean against the driver's door and greeting each driver courteously. Of course everyone knows the reason they lean in like that is to engage you in conversation so they can smell your breath, study your pupils and speech, and assess whether or not you've been drinking. Naturally anyone who has been drinking, which is just about everyone who is passing through there on a Friday night, admits to having had "two beers." They seem to think this will give them some kind of credibility and that the troopers haven't heard that line at least fifty million times already that night. Me, I never say such a stupid thing.

"Good evening, ma'am," the trooper said through lips that were hidden beneath the typical macho mustache all-male law-enforcement personnel seem compelled to grow. "Had anything to drink tonight?"

"No, sir," I answered confidently with just a hint of boredom, as I looked directly into his eyes. That's always the key, a hint of boredom and direct eye contact.

"Okay, ma'am," he said, obviously convinced that I was not a danger to society. "Sorry for the inconvenience," he added, handing me a pamphlet with a graph on it that mapped out how many drinks I could have at my weight and not end up in jail. "This is just a sobriety checkpoint for everyone's safety," he explained. "You have a nice night now." He smiled, though I half expected a salute.

With that, he made some kind of hand signal to the trooper up ahead to let me through, and I gave him one more bored smile as I slowly drove on. I passed two more troopers who waved me on, and I slowly accelerated once the red flares were a fading image in my rearview mirror.

Then a funny thing happened.

I thought I saw a man on a motorcycle blocking my lane just a short distance up ahead. I figured it must be another cop, since the troopers were right behind me and surely they would never have permitted any ordinary person to sit there without concluding there was a problem. Like a drunk driver.

This was getting tiresome. I thought I'd already proved myself to the troopers behind me. What could they possibly want now? I rolled my eyes as I got close enough for him to see my exasperation and simultaneously rolled the window down. "Now what?" I demanded loudly enough for him to hear over the short distance that separated us in the muggy, steamy night.

"A bit defensive tonight, aren't we?" he commented as he dismounted his motorcycle and walked toward my car. I couldn't tell if his words had been sarcastic or just observant, but something didn't feel right. His face was hidden in the shadow of his motorcycle helmet and in a terrifying flash of awareness, I realized he wasn't wearing any kind of uniform or badge and that the bike he was riding was a Harley-Davidson. Cool as they may think they are, I know that New Jersey state troopers do not ride Harley-Davidsons, at least not on duty. Red flags went up all over my brain and railroad gates came crashing down in my mind with flashing red lights that signaled "Danger! Danger! Danger!" I knew he was an impostor, yet I refused to let my terror

33

show. Of course, it's easy to be brave when you know that there are at least a dozen state troopers within screaming distance.

That's when I noticed that he looked somewhat familiar. Was he maybe some old boyfriend of mine? Or an old wanna-be boyfriend who had heard I was back in town this week? Who *was* this guy? There was definitely something familiar about him, but I couldn't quite put my finger on it. Then it hit me. This was the guy who had stopped my panic attack earlier that night, the guy I'd been watching for and hoping would come back. Now here he was, in the flesh, staring down at me, and once again putting me completely at ease with his amiable grin. But what was he doing here? In the middle of the road? In the middle of the night?

Living on the West Coast for the last few years hadn't changed me much. I automatically lapsed into my hard-edged, sarcastic, East Coast demeanor even though I was immensely attracted to the guy. "Can I help you?" I said, purposely snapping my gum in the most obnoxious, uncaring manner I could muster.

"I'm not the one who needs help," he said, chuckling.

"Excoooose me?" I bantered, a little off balance from the remark.

"I'm Joe," he offered politely, extending his right hand toward my driver's side window for an introductory handshake. Somehow he managed not to invade my personal space in the process, and that surprised me. I'm very sensitive to that sort of thing, being in my line of work and all. In fact, I have very good instincts about most things, and I always listen to my intuition. Nature may have short-changed women on sheer physical, muscular strength, but she made up for it by giving us two secret weapons: intelligence and gut instincts. For some strange reason, my gut instincts were telling me to trust this man. But wait a minute, I'd never trusted *any* man, so why did I want to trust this one?

"Follow your instincts," Joe said softly. "You can trust me."

35

I was flabbergasted. Why had he said that? Surely he couldn't read my mind. I wouldn't put that talent past a woman of course, but I don't know any men who are that highly evolved. Usually they can't understand us even if we use sign language, flip charts, and a megaphone.

"Heather, try to relax." He smiled warmly. "I'm not here to hurt you."

"Relax?" I said. "Relax? Hey! How did you know my name?" I knew that was a dumb move the moment I said it.

"There's no need to be afraid of me," he murmured softly. "Rest assured that I will never hurt you. I'm here only because this is where I'm supposed to be right now and so are you. Our whole encounter is perfect, just the way it's supposed to be. Do you understand that?"

"What the heck are you talking about?" I demanded, not even trying to make sense of his words.

"Maybe I'm getting a little ahead of myself," he said contritely. "But trust me, Heather. You have nothing to fear."

I wished he'd quit using my name like that. It spooked me every time he said it. "Well, then, if we're all exactly where we're supposed to be, why aren't you in some biker bar guzzling brewskies instead of blocking traffic right here in front of a dozen troopers?" I said it with utter confidence, hoping to avoid a deep conversation about his "perfect encounter" theory.

He glanced behind me toward the red flares and the occupied troopers. "There's nothing to worry about," he said almost sadly. "They can't see me."

"Well, they will if I scream," I said threateningly.

"But you won't scream," he replied with absolute confidence.

"Who *are* you?" I pleaded, surprised at the urgency I heard in my voice.

He smiled softly, but he didn't answer.

"I am going to scream," I warned, hoping for a reaction, any reaction, from him.

"Suit yourself," he murmured absently.

I really didn't want to scream. I'd had enough of those troopers already, and for some reason, I was fairly certain this "Joe" character didn't pose any danger to me, though I didn't know how I knew that. "Why do you say they can't see you?" I asked, suddenly remembering what he'd said three sentences ago and realizing that it appeared to be true.

"Because they only look for what's wrong in people," he answered nonchalantly. "It's not their fault," he added quickly. "It's just their job. You know, weeding out the bad guys and bringing them to justice." He lowered his eyes. "If that's what you call it," he added somberly.

"You still haven't answered my question," I insisted. "Why can't they see you and your big old Harley taking up space in the middle of the road while traffic has to go around you?"

He didn't answer right away, and that gave me time to think about what he'd just said. "Well, if the cops only look for the bad side of people," I pondered aloud, "and you claim they can't see *you,* then you must be some kind of superhuman who has no faults. Is that what you're saying?" My comment was mostly sarcastic, but he took it very seriously.

"Something like that," he answered pensively. "I'm not crazy about the word 'super' though. There's no need for it. We're all exactly who we are, and that should be good enough. No one needs to be a 'super' anything." A patient smile crossed his lips then, and he looked over his shoulder at the troopers, then back at me. "The point is that when you only look for what's bad in people, eventually that's all you see. That's what makes cops burn out at such an early age."

"You're serious, aren't you?" I asked, a bit incredulous. Who *was* this guy?

"I don't want to overwhelm you, Heather, by telling you who I am." His voice was kind, and the gentle curve of his mouth made his words even more intriguing than his tone.

We were both silent for a moment, each for our own reasons. Then his face brightened and he suggested trying an experiment. Where had I heard that line before?

"No, this is harmless," he said, an irresistible spark of enthusiasm in his dark mahogany eyes.

Before I could protest, he was telling me to count all the New York license plates that went by among the next dozen cars that passed us. Being as this was a summer resort town and there were always plenty of New Yorkers around on Friday nights, I humored him. I was surprised to count only three though, and I wondered if maybe the Bennies had found a new haven, not that I would miss them.

"Only three," I announced triumphantly. "Three New Yorkers. What do I win?"

"We're not done yet," he said. "How many Pennsylvania tags did you see?"

"What?" I said, surprised. "No fair! You didn't tell me to watch for Pennsy plates. Only New Yorkers," I whined.

"I know," he said with a knowing smile. "But now I'm asking how many Pennsylvania tags went by."

I sat there with my mouth hanging wide open. "I don't know," I answered, gathering my composure. "How could I possibly know? I wasn't watching for them. What's this all about anyway?'' I demanded.

"Sometimes when you look really hard for one thing, that's the *only* thing you see," he said, brown eyes beaming some kind of invisible, yet intense energy into mine. "Then you miss all the other things going on around you," he finished.

I was speechless for a moment, trying to absorb the magnitude of what I had just witnessed in myself.

41

"That's why those state troopers can't see me," he added patiently. "They're not *looking* for me. In fact, a lot of them don't even think I exist."

Now I really was afraid. Suddenly I had an inkling of who this guy might be, and that was very, very scary to someone like me who never believed he existed. I still resisted the very thought of it, even if I was hearing it straight from the horse's mouth. "Give it to me straight," I urged. "Who *are* you?"

He studied me for a long moment while the late-night coastal clouds parted as if on cue, exposing a hazy, yellow moon, which now cast an inviting saffron glow onto the deserted beach.

"Maybe you'd better pull over there," Joe said, pointing to a vacant parking lot by the beach. "It's a long story."

3

I PULLED INTO THE DARK-
ened parking lot and killed the lights. Joe
pulled his Hog around behind my rented
Camaro and gracefully dismounted, removing
his helmet in one swift, well-practiced movement.

He sauntered up to my driver's side window
again, and I liked that he didn't automatically
assume he was invited into the passenger
seat. I know I didn't verbalize that feeling, but
he addressed my unspoken remark anyway. "I

never go anywhere that I'm not invited," he said, grinning.

I smiled tenuously. I honestly didn't know what to make of him. Part of me knew beyond a doubt who he was, but still, I was unable to accept it. Just thinking about it frightened me so much that I began to sense the beginnings of another panic attack.

"I'm sorry," he said. "I don't mean to upset you." He pulled one hand out of his jeans pocket and held it out to me. "Here," he said, "hold my hand."

I looked at his graceful, outstretched hand as if it were a pipe bomb.

"Go ahead," he implored, emanating something incredibly beautiful and trustworthy from the depths of his dark eyes. "I promise you'll feel better."

Mutely, I watched as my left hand took on a life of its own and slid inside his large, open palm. He hesitated for only a moment, then curled his long, graceful fingers around my tightly gripped fist. His massive hand was a sanctuary, a safe and lovely refuge to me, and I was enveloped by a cloud of serenity that started in my fingertips and traveled up the length of my arm, calming my pounding heart and tranquilizing my frenzied brain.

"Who *are* you?" I whispered for the third time. I'd had enough of this guessing game. What I needed was for him to come right out and say it.

He sealed our entwined fingers with his other hand, and I thought I might die from the sheer peace I felt. "I am the mother ship," he said softly into the night, "the wheel in which you are a prized and valuable spoke, the delicate gold necklace of the universe in which you are a precious and necessary link."

No man had ever spoken such poetry to me, and I was mesmerized. I wanted to cry and to laugh at the same time. I wanted to sing and dance and melt into him all at once. I wanted to *be* him. But wait a minute! Get a grip! I chided myself

"What are you saying?" I demanded. "You . . . you're not, well . . . What are you saying?" I repeated.

"It's true, Heather," he murmured. "I am who you think I am."

"Who?" I demanded in my most doubtful, accusing tone, though something deep in a long-forgotten corner of my being already knew the answer, but was too terrified to admit it.

He was silent for a long moment. "You tell me," he offered gently. "It's stronger that way."

"Oh, God," was all I could say.

"That's very good," he murmured sweetly.

"No," I shot back, still ready for a fight, still afraid of playing the fool. "No way, pal. Ever heard of a little thing called 'delusions of grandeur'?" I taunted in my most sarcastic East Coast tone. "They have drugs for it now, I hear. Just check yourself into some psychiatric clinic or something. Really," I continued, "they can help you."

"Heather," he said softly.

"Really, I'm not kidding," I insisted. "They've made great strides in that field. Honestly." It was no use. He wasn't buying it. And neither was I.

"Heather," he said again, his voice soft as the early morning breeze.

"Oh, God, what?" I said, scared out of my mind. I mean, an assailant I could maybe fight off. A drunk, I could maybe convince to leave me alone. But God himself? How do you respond to that? Nothing in my life had prepared me for this.

"It doesn't require preparation." He grinned at me affably.

"Look, why me?" I begged lamely. "What could you possibly want with me? I'm no one important."

"You wouldn't be here if you weren't important," he whispered.

I've always been a firm believer in laying my cards on the table, especially when the deck is stacked against me. I may have been accused of a lot of things in my life, but being a shrinking violet has never been one of them. I take pride in shooting straight from the hip, and this was not going to be an exception. "Look, uh, uh—I don't know what to call you," I said, suddenly befuddled.

"*Joe* is fine," he said patiently.

"Yeah, well, Joe," I said, trying to regain some trace of my former composure, "I don't think I'm the right person for whatever it is you have in mind. Maybe you should just, ya know, shine me on, dude."

" 'Dude'?" he asked.

"Jeez, you're a little sensitive, don't you think?"

He laughed at that. "Believe me, if I were the sensitive type, I'd have died several million times by now," he assured me. "The thing is, Heather, it's about time we straightened out a few things in your life. I'm here to help fix the things that are hurting you. Try to believe that."

"Well, if you really are God," I challenged, "why didn't you come to me as a woman? It would have made it a lot easier for me to trust you right from the start."

"I am a woman," he answered with a straight face.

"Yeah, and I'm E.T.," I said mockingly.

"No, really," he insisted. "I *am* a woman. I'm a man too, if that's what you want me to be."

"What?" I scowled.

"I'm whatever you want me to be. People

48

who think I'm a man aren't any more correct than people who think I'm a woman. Actually they're both different sides of the same coin. And I am *all* things, so I am both man and woman at the same time. Get it?"

"No," I said bluntly.

"You will," he answered calmly. "But on some basic level, you must perceive me as a man, because that's what I'm picking up from you, and I usually come to people in a form that I know they have been conditioned to accept. It's just to help you relate, but in the overall scheme of things, it's neither here nor there."

49

"Then why don't you cut us women a break and wear a dress once in a while?" I retorted. "It would do wonders for our credibility." I still could not fathom that I was talking to the Almighty himself, hence my defensive irreverence.

He seemed to consider that, then concluded, "Pants are just a lot more practical."

I opened my mouth to speak, but he cut me off with a teasing smile and added, "Besides, enlightening the world is a tough job, and things being what they are, people still tend to listen to men a little more readily. I'm not saying it's fair, but I have my work cut out for me, so I had to give myself every advantage. You understand, don't you?"

"No, I don't understand," I insisted. "It seems to me, you've given most of the advantages to men all along," I continued, my hand automatically going to my hip in a stance of righteous indignation. "When is it ever going to be *our* turn?"

"Your turn?" he asked, an amused smile on his lips and one eyebrow raised. "Your turn for what?"

"Our turn to have the advantages in life, you know, the power, the money, the freedom. Stuff like that. Stuff that men have had since time began."

"I see," he said, turning his glance to the moonlit beach and the gentle waves of low tide. He was silent for a long moment, and I began to sense victory. I figured if he had had a good answer for the fact that women have historically been treated like second-class citizens, he would have offered it by now. Naturally, my assumption of triumph was premature.

He squatted down on the asphalt beside my car, picked up a broken clam shell, and examined it absently in the light from the distant streetlamp. "You make it sound like men and women are on opposing teams," he said, his voice tinged with weariness or perhaps sadness.

"Well, of course we are," I answered readily, but his somber tone disturbed me for some reason. "Look," I offered, "I have a theory about men and women. Want to hear it?"

He looked up at me, dark eyes engulfing me in a cloud of warmth, and for a moment I was mesmerized by the magnificence of his face. Why had it taken me so long to notice how incredibly handsome he was? And why was I suddenly filled with such a sense of utter trust in this man?

"I want to hear everything you say, Heather," he said softly, "every thought that floats through your consciousness, every dream that invades your sleep, every one of your heart's desires. Tell me, Heather. Tell me what's on your mind."

I was momentarily dumbfounded, and the kindness of his words had the reverse effect on me. I didn't remember anyone ever being this interested in something I had to say. In fact, it had always been just the opposite. All of my life it seems I've been told that I say too much, that I should not be so opinionated, that I should learn to control my tongue. Now this man was truly interested, truly wanted to hear what I was thinking, and I was speechless.

"Dígame," he urged, his voice slightly above a whisper.

"That's Spanish," I announced, wondering why he used a foreign language to entice me to speak to him. "I know what it means too," I added proudly.

"Of course you do." He smiled. "And you know far more than even you realize. Speak to me, Heather," he repeated, this time in English. "What is your theory that you were going to tell me?"

"Well, you see, I believe all women were men in a former life."

"Oh?" he said, tilting his head to the side.

"Definitely," I continued. "That's why we tolerate men. It's kind of like the fact that all adults were once children, so that's why they can be patient and tolerant with their own kids, because adults know how it was when *they* were kids."

He nodded his head as though digesting what I was saying.

"So, you see," I went on, "all females were probably men in a previous life, and then they evolved into a more mature gender called women. That's why women can be patient— well, sometimes—and try to teach men how to be civilized like us. It doesn't always work of course, but just like an adult guardian, we have a responsibility to set a good example."

"I see," he said, absently tracing the line of his square jaw. "You've obviously given this a lot of thought."

I don't know what came over me just then, but I suddenly had a yen to take a moonlight stroll on the beach. Go figure. Me, the most streetwise person I know. Me, Hard-hearted Hannah of the nineties, wanting to hike barefoot along the cool, wet sand, holding the hand of a man who spoke to me in Spanish and in the universal language of the heart. A man who knew I had dreams and who encouraged me to describe them.

He rose to his feet just then and opened my car door, offering his hand and gesturing for me to step out of the car. I don't know how he knew what I had been thinking, but it didn't seem to matter. A heavy weight that had been riding on my shoulders for years now, like the proverbial albatross around my neck, suddenly evaporated. I felt wispy and light, which is no small feat for someone who is five feet ten in stocking feet and who has far more muscle mass than the average female.

"Why do I feel so light?" I asked in amazement as he slid the key from the ignition and locked the door as he closed it.

"The fear has left you," he said matter-of-factly.

"The fear? What fear?" I asked, still caught

up in my need for a tough, East Coast facade of boldness.

He just chuckled and grasped my hand, his fingers completely engulfing mine and leaving me to feel small and fragile in his presence. Actually, it wasn't a bad feeling at all. Different maybe, since no man had ever made me feel small, being as I'm taller than the average guy and probably in better shape too. Funny though, I sort of liked the feeling.

"You'll get used to it," he said, smiling. He led me over the boulders that line the edge of the beach to help prevent erosion during Jersey's severe winter storms. I'd foolishly neglected to wear my contact lenses that night, so I could hardly see where I was going on the dark, rocky beach, yet I was too vain to whip out my glasses. I'd rather break my ankle than have any man see me with my glasses on.

He laughed out loud, and I knew he had somehow read my mind again. The funny thing was that suddenly I was able to laugh at myself, and that was certainly a new sensation. Somehow I knew Joe was a man who spoke the language of all people, who knew everyone's deepest and best-kept secrets, and that nothing I could say or do would surprise him or put him off. Still though, I had my pride. I wasn't about to look at him through the Coke-bottle lenses of my horn-rimmed glasses.

Fortunately, he was as surefooted on those giant rocks as the donkeys who give rides to tourists down into the bowels of the Grand Canyon.

56

"You've been there?" he asked, an amused smile in his voice. "To the Grand Canyon?"

"Once," I replied, too preoccupied with keeping my balance on the slippery rocks to notice that he seemed to be reading my mind again. He descended onto the beach, then gallantly placed his hands around my waist and lifted me gently onto the sand beside him.

"Good," he said, releasing my waist and reaching for my hand again. "Too few people have been there, and it's one of those places I purposely created so no one would forget me." He was silent for a long moment then. "Did you like it there?" he finally asked.

"Yeah, it was okay," I answered absently.

"Just 'okay'?" he said, unable to hide the surprise in his voice. "I would have thought you'd be a little more in awe," he added, a hint of hurt creeping into his tone.

"Oh, don't go getting all offended," I chided. "It was nice. Kind of beautiful, actually," I conceded.

"Not as beautiful as you." He smiled admiringly. "Human spirits are the most beautiful of all my creations," he added, eyes sweeping the star-studded sky, "and yet they are almost always unhappy with their physical appearance."

I was caught off guard for a moment by that statement, but I made a quick and typical recovery. "Well, I know you're not talking about me," I countered. "I work hard for this body and I'm quite proud of it," I finished smugly.

"That's exactly what I'm talking about," he

said, coming to a dead halt. He gazed silently for a moment into my eyes, then removed the black leather motorcycle jacket and spread it out as far as it would go on the cool sand. He lowered his lanky frame onto the sand and patted the jacket beside him, beckoning me to sit there. "The whole reason I made your body with all of its complexities and backup systems is so that you would never *have* to think about it. I wanted you to spend your time thinking about more important things, like learning to be kind to one another and evolving to your fullest potential." His eyes softened then, and he added, "Your body is only a container for your spirit. It's your spiritual essence that defines you, not your body."

"Yeah, well, what could be more important than thinking about your body?" I asked defiantly. "Without my body, what else have I got?" Let him try and answer that one, I thought.

"Oh, Heather," he sighed sadly. "I thought people, especially women, had moved far beyond that narrow concept of beauty."

"Hey, I got news for you, pal," I countered.

"It's not women who define beauty in this world, in case you haven't noticed."

He looked out at the blackness of the ocean for a long time without saying anything. For a fleeting moment, I wondered if maybe my emphasis on having a perfect body, and demanding nothing less from the men in my life, might be just a bit shallow.

"How long have you lived in southern California now?" he asked in a tone that was nothing but kindness and sincere interest.

"Five years."

"And what was the reason you went there in the first place?" he asked gently. "What was it you were looking for?"

I thought hard before I spoke. For some reason, it seemed important for me to give an utterly honest answer. Somehow I knew that what I said would reveal something about myself that I had never considered before. I knew I was about to flick on a light in some obscure and darkened corner of my soul, and I was afraid of what I might find there. What if I stumbled upon the feelings that I had purposely never sat still long enough to examine?

That's when an image popped into my mind, and I immediately knew how to explain why I'd packed everything I owned five years ago and had headed west.

"Well, it's like this," I began. "About five years ago, someone got the brilliant idea to build a miniature golf course along the beach here. They wanted to make it real exotic and stuff, so they imported palm trees from South America and planted them around the perimeter of the course."

He turned his splendid face to me and seemed enraptured by my story.

"Well, the summer was great," I went on. "All the Bennies and Shoe-bees and the rest of the summer tourists just thought it was the cat's pajamas having palm trees on the famous Jersey shore. It was suddenly the poor man's vacation, you know?"

"And?" he murmured softly.

"Well, of course, eventually winter reared its ugly head and all the palm trees died as soon as the first frost hit. I mean, didn't they *know* that was gonna happen? Were they really stupid enough to think that palm trees would survive an East Coast winter?''

"So how did that make you decide to move to the West Coast?" he asked earnestly, not even a trace of impatience in his voice.

"Well, I used to jog past there every morning and look at those poor dying palm trees, and after a while, I began to realize that I was a lot like them.''

He cocked an eyebrow but said nothing.

"I realized that *I* was dying too," I continued. "I felt so trapped. I was waiting tables just down the road from here at Vinnie's Diner, and I was just dying inside. Somehow I knew that I was in the wrong environment. That I could never blossom here on this fast-paced, freezing cold, dog-eat-dog East Coast.''

"So you listened to the yearnings in your heart and went to the placc that you fclt was somehow gentler and freer," he finished for me.

"Yeah," I said, amazed at his capacity to understand. "Yeah."

He was quiet a moment longer, then slid

that now familiar protective arm around me. It felt particularly good this time. "Your intentions were so pure," he mused.

"What do you mean *were?*" I challenged, ready for any kind of a fight he wanted to start.

"Nothing." He smiled. "California has one of the best attitudes I've seen in a long time. It's just that a lot of people seem to have gotten a little carried away with that search for the perfect body. They started out with pure intentions just like you, wanting to have fun and to enjoy life. But somewhere along the way, they lost track of fun and started judging people by how 'buff' they could make their bodies."

There was nothing I could say. The man had definitely made a good point.

He noticed my speechlessness and added, "Rebels are my favorite people, Heather. Did you know that?"

"Are you calling me a rebel?" I challenged.

"I try to stay away from labels; they're dangerous," he admonished. "But I know that deep in your heart you consider yourself a rebel and that you're kind of proud of that. You've spent a lot of time being angry about the injustices of your past and trying to remove yourself from them, and there's nothing wrong with that." He studied me silently for only a heartbeat, then added softly, "It's just that you've been running in the wrong direction."

I definitely didn't want to talk about the past, about my miserable childhood and all the pain it had caused me. I simply wasn't ready to churn up all those old feelings, so I just sat there quietly. Why beat a dead horse?

Joe sighed softly then and got to his feet. Towering over me, he extended his large hand and gently pulled me up to face him, and in spite of the midsummer heat wave, goose bumps appeared once again on my arms. A knowing smile crossed his lips as he plucked the black leather jacket from the sand and draped it across my shoulders. "I can see we have a lot of material to cover," he said,

63

smiling. "I hope you don't mind if I run into you again and continue this conversation."

"Suit yourself," I said, secretly amazed at the vague sense of disappointment I felt that he was bringing our encounter to a close, though of course, I chose not to show it. "Before we leave though," I insisted, "tell me what's so bad about being a rebel."

His smile spread to his eyes then and his words were like melted butter. "Nothing," he replied, his tone soft as a kiss. "Rebels are the truth seekers of the universe," he said lovingly. "People who aren't oppressed, don't rebel. That's why I save only the toughest challenges for the people I know have the courage to question the status quo and who eventually make the world see things differently. Hopefully, they are the same people who help the world to change, preferably in a nonviolent way."

"Are you saying that you approve of me?" I asked, incredulous that anyone, especially some spiritual guy like this, could appreciate someone like me. "Aren't you going to criticize me for my lifestyle? For being, well, you know, a . . . uh, stripper?"

He laughed softly, then tilted my chin so that I had no choice but to fall into the warmth of his engulfing brown eyes.

"My dear sweet Heather," he whispered, "you have no idea how I cherish you."

4

*T*HE REST OF MY VACATION was uneventful after that. Well, how can you compare *anything* to the company I'd shared that night on the beach? In fact, I didn't even remember driving home that night. I guess my brain just went on automatic pilot, and come to think of it, I'd been in a sort of trance ever since. I mean, if this guy really was who he said he was, he obviously had no interest in passing judgment on me. And I don't have to tell you what a relief *that* was. In fact, he had acknowledged that it takes courage to ask questions. He had even called me a "truth seeker," and suddenly I had a sense of myself that no amount of bodybuilding had ever given me.

In a way, I kind of felt sorry for him. I thought he got a bum rap here on earth. I mean, it seems people have always depicted God as some very narrow-minded, judgmental being who delights in dishing out his version of justice. But if everyone could spend just one moonlit hour on the beach with him like I did, they would see that nothing could be farther from the truth. The man apparently had been totally misunderstood, and I could certainly relate to that.

On the day of my departure, my only regret was that I hadn't run into him again before my vacation ended. I'd gone out of my way to hang out in the places where I first met him, but it was as though he had disappeared off the face of the earth. I kept hanging on to the fact that he had alluded to future conversations with me, but I had a two PM flight that day for LA, so I didn't hold out much hope.

I have always preferred physical labor to mental calisthenics. I'd rather move a mountain than solve a problem any day. My idea of hell is having to think at all, and it's not because I'm dumb or anything like that; it's just that I suppose my parents and my grade-school teachers may have been right. I'm "mentally lazy." Yet, surprisingly, Joe had made the whole thinking process not only painless but enjoyable, and I was fascinated. I only wished we had talked more about my future and about my goal of being a Vegas lounge singer. I wondered what advice he would have given me.

None of that mattered now. My vacation was over and I had to get back to LA. I supposed I might never see him again, and I decided to be grateful for having spent even that one hour with him. How many people could claim that? Not that I had any intention of telling anyone. I told you I'm not dumb.

I turned in my rented Camaro at Newark Airport and headed for my direct flight to LA. I didn't look forward to going back to work at the club later that night, but it would be nice to get back to the familiar refuge of my condo. If Nick, the Pink Pussycat's owner, and Anthony, his weasel of a son, thought I had attitude *before* this vacation, they had better watch out now. I had something that went beyond "buff." God or "Joe" or whoever he was had said he cherished me, and what could be more empowering than that?

I checked my bags and thought I recognized the skycap as the same one who had taken them for me at the baggage claim when I arrived. It was hard to tell at first because he kept his head down. "Are you sure this is all, ma'am?" he mumbled as he loaded my luggage onto a cart.

I was busy digging through my wallet for some singles and distractedly said, "Yeah, why?"

"I remember this luggage," he said. "You don't see too many flamingo pink ones. Seems to me you had more when you got here, though. You sure you didn't leave a bag somewhere?"

"Yeah, I'm sure," I said, a little annoyed that this skycap suddenly thought he was my mother. No doubt he was just looking for a bigger tip.

He had his back to me when he spoke, but his voice was achingly familiar. "You see how you are?" he teased. "Always the rebel."

"Joe," I breathed, wide-eyed, and waited for him to turn around.

"Fact is, you did leave some baggage behind." He grinned, turning to face me and swallowing me in those enormous, brown velvet eyes. "It may not have been flamingo pink, but I'd venture to say you're feeling a lot less burdened without it."

I was aghast. "What are you doing here? . . . How did you . . . ? Was that really *you* when I first got here?"

He stood there grinning at me, thoroughly enjoying my embarrassment. "You didn't think I'd let you go without saying good-bye, did you?"

"Come with me!" I suddenly urged. I was just beginning to realize that this man was capable of creating any situation he wanted to.

"I have every intention of coming with

you," he said seriously. "Just try losing me. It's impossible."

"Well, we better hurry if we're going to get you a ticket," I foolishly suggested. "My flight departs in a few minutes."

"It doesn't work like that," he said, placing both hands gently on my shoulders. "One of the privileges of being who I am is not having to sit in those tiny, cramped seats for over five hours," he said, grinning. He brought his right forefinger to his lips, planted a kiss on the tip, then placed it softly over my lips. "I'll see you when you get out there, California Dreamer." He smiled. "Have a good trip."

With that, he turned and faded into the fast-forwarded crowd of the chaotic airport. I stood for a long time pressing my fingers to that place on my lips, mesmerized as much by his touch as by the cloud of serenity he seemed to leave in his wake. When I finally took my fingers from my lips, there was a piece of silver glitter on one of them.

It wasn't until a woman pushing a baby stroller ran over my toes as she barreled toward her gate that I remembered I had a plane to catch. Clutching my carry-on bag, I got to the gate just as my plane was boarding.

Settled comfortably in a window seat, I had time to sit back and reflect quietly on all that had happened on my vacation. Not surprisingly, there had been all the usual tensions and nitpicking that have gone on in my family for as long as I can remember. They all think I make my living as a makeup artist to the stars, and I do nothing to discourage that image. Naturally, we argued, criticized, and accused each other of all kinds of misdeeds and shortcomings while I was home, just like old times. Old, *miserable* times. But I've learned a few survival tactics over the years, and now I don an invisible coat of armor that doesn't allow the craziness to get to me. When the end of my visit mercifully arrives, we sweep our differences under the rug, kiss good-bye, and try to act like normal people till the next time I visit and the cycle begins again. It doesn't even faze me anymore.

What did faze me, however, was the fact that I had met God, himself, on this vacation.

If I had doubted it at first, I was absolutely certain of it now, and that struck me as very funny. If I were God, I think the last person on earth I would hang out with would be me.

I stopped believing in God when I was in the second grade at Our Lady of Sorrows Catholic grammar school. I remember how the nuns used to drag us into church every day during Lent and how we used to have to sit there quietly, praying and atoning for our sins.

Inevitably, I would run out of sins to atone for, even though Sister Mary Margaret said that was impossible. I would just sit there staring at the murals painted on the walls and the ceiling, scaring myself to death, which I suppose was better than boring myself to death by atoning. Those pictures were absolutely horrifying to a six-year-old.

There was this one painting of all these people who were burning in hell for their sins. Apparently they were naked, but all you could see were their bare arms reaching up from the white-hot inferno and their agonized faces begging for mercy as flames licked their

73

charred bodies. Sometimes if I listened really carefully, I could swear I actually heard them screaming. Those pictures spooked me for years, and to this day, they sometimes haunt my dreams. That's why, at the age of six, it was easier to believe that there really wasn't a God, just a bunch of weird people who paint pictures on church walls to terrify little kids into behaving themselves. Apparently, it doesn't always work.

Now, here was God, hanging out on the beach with me, patiently teaching me some of the things Sister Mary Margaret had tried to beat into me. Not only did I find myself suddenly believing in God after all these years, but I was falling a little bit in love with him to boot. *That* ought to cost me some major penance. I just hoped I wouldn't end up depicted in a mural on some church wall.

It was late afternoon when I landed in Los Angeles, thanks to the three-hour time difference. I made my way to the baggage claim at the chaotic LAX, absently reading limo drivers' signs with peoples names written with black felt-tip pens. I always figured if I had a kid someday, this would be a good way to pick out a name, since there's such a variety.

I stood at the number three carousel, watching the array of luggage circle the travel-weary crowd. I noticed one particularly beat-up-looking bag go by at least three times without anyone claiming it, and I found myself almost overcome with sympathy for it. That's exactly how I had felt so many times in my life, like a leftover suitcase that just keeps going around and around, hoping someone will save it from its endless, circular journey.

Shrugging off that depressing thought, I spotted my two pink bags and hoisted them onto the rental cart beside me. Heading toward the long-term parking lot, my luggage in tow, I noticed one of those handwritten placards with *my* name on it. I blinked and looked again, and sure enough, "Heather Hurley," it read.

I recognized the long graceful hands holding the sign, even before I noticed the familiar jeans and T-shirt and high-top sneakers. I no longer needed to see Joe's face to recognize him because every inch of him was undeniably "Joe." There he stood, in the middle of the LAX, smiling from ear to ear as he watched my astonished reaction.

"I hope you don't plan to strap my luggage to your Harley," I quipped, trying to contain the utter joy that was fluttering around in my heart.

"I don't like to draw that much attention to myself," he answered seriously. "I figured we'd take your car," he said, tossing the placard with my name on it into the nearby garbage bin. "That was just so I wouldn't miss you."

In an unlikely fit of affection, I blurted out, "Well, I *did* miss you in a way."

He just smiled and wrapped a strong arm around me while he pushed my cart with the other. "I know you have to work tonight," he went on, without even a trace of the disapproval I was half expecting. "But I thought I'd keep you company on the way home, if you don't mind."

If I don't mind?! If I don't mind?! Didn't he know how thrilled I was to see him again? I smiled up at him and realized by the smug grin on his face, that of course he knew.

When we reached the car, Joe took the keys from me and deftly loaded my luggage into the trunk, then opened the passenger door for me. "Okay with you if I drive?" he asked.

It was more than okay as far as I was concerned. Ordinarily I would never let a man slip so casually into my car or into my life, but with Joe it felt like the most natural thing in the world. Somehow I never felt like he was intruding on me or invading my privacy. I had never felt this comfortable with a man before, and I liked the feeling.

We talked and laughed the whole way home, and by the time we pulled into the garage beneath my condo, I desperately did not want to work tonight. "All good things must come to an end, I suppose," I muttered softly as I let myself out of the car and noticed Joe's Harley parked in the guest parking space.

"That's not necessarily true," Joe replied nonchalantly, lifting my bags from the trunk. "All the good things are here, right this very minute, just waiting to *begin*. Waiting for you to discover them."

I stared blankly at him for a moment until

the ring of the elevator startled me into speech. "Yeah, well, the good things will have to wait till I get off work tonight," I said sadly. "I don't suppose there are too many wondrous moments waiting for me there."

"You have a choice you know, Heather," he said quietly.

"Oh, don't start that," I retorted defensively. "If I don't work, I don't survive. It's as simple as that, and I don't really feel like talking about it right now," I added, taking my bags from him and dropping them inside the waiting elevator.

He smiled gently and placed his long, graceful hand on the elevator door, preventing it from closing. "When *would* you like to talk about it?" he asked sincerely.

"Never," I grunted.

"How about tomorrow?" he asked pleasantly. "We could go to the beach on my Harley. The beach is always a great place for important talks, don't you think?"

"What I think," I answered impatiently, "is that I'm going to be late for work if I don't get upstairs and unpack some of this stuff right this minute."

"You're right," he agreed. "You'll be late for something that you hate, and you wouldn't want to do that."

I studied him for a hint of criticism or impatience in his tone but found none. He was only speaking the truth. The truth that I wasn't willing to hear just yet.

"Look, I don't have time to argue," I insisted. "I'll see you around, okay?"

His smile widened then, and he looked at me knowingly. "I'll pick you up at noon," he said with a wink, "and bring your bathing suit." He sauntered toward his bike, and I heard the laughter in his voice as he called over his shoulder, "Surf's up, dude."

5

HE MINUTE I PULLED INTO the rear parking lot and let myself in the backstage door, it was as though I had never left this joint. Going back to work is always hard I suppose, but for some reason it seemed more difficult than usual. As much as I hated to admit it, a week of summer frolic on the Jersey shore had left me with a bit of a hole in my heart. Not that I had any desire to return to my old lifestyle of that dead-end waitressing job at Vinnie's Diner and dating the same old recycled crowd of losers. It's just that for the past week at least, I hadn't given a thought to pleasing anyone but myself, and it was depressing to know it was over now. The only thing that made any of it bearable was the fact that Joe was here and every moment spent with him was like another mini-vacation.

I knew that the minute I stepped up on stage tonight, I would have to go back to disassociating my mind from my body and simply go through the motions of entertaining the crowd. Not that I mind wearing seductive little outfits and strutting my stuff around a well-guarded stage while men drool over me. House rules dictate that they can look all they want, but they can't touch, so in a way it's an ideal situation. The only thing that gets stroked is my ego, and that's fine with me. It's just that sometimes I'm not even in the mood to have my ego stroked either. Sometimes it would just be nice to have a choice, and despite what Joe had said earlier about my having choices, I wasn't certain he really understood what it takes to survive on this planet.

Don't get me wrong. They pay us extremely well to prance around half naked in this smoky, dimly lit, and well-guarded atmosphere, to say nothing of the "tips" that are routinely stuffed into the garters on our well-toned thighs. Of course, some of us make better tips than others, depending on how good we look and how provocative a fantasy we can sell them. I don't like to brag, but on a good night I've been known to make both the mortgage and the car payment.

It costs my clients an extra hundred bucks if they want a private "table dance" from me. That's when I come down off the stage (or the "meat rack," as we strippers call it) and perform a slow, sensual number on their table, where they can get up close and look at the perfection of my body. Not every dancer can charge that much, but since I am the most requested performer, Nick, the owner, says it's good for business. Besides, he splits the fee with me.

Getting men to believe in a fantasy, that's what my job's all about. Even so, I'm always surprised at the number of "clients" who are actually very intelligent, successful business-men in the real world, but who are easily led down the primrose path when you start play-ing fantasy games. Thank God for testoster-one. When you add alcohol to it, the result is rather predictable . . . and profitable.

So here I was, backstage at the club, my first night back from vacation, agonizing over which outfit would suit my fancy tonight. I couldn't decide, so I did my makeup first in the incredibly harsh lights that surround the mirrors in our paltry little dressing room. Only a sadist would have invented lights like these, probably the same guy who designed the lighting in the dressing rooms of most department stores.

Anyway, I continued to study and correct every little facial flaw with makeup, hoping that the face I painted on would somehow inspire me toward a creative and seductive performance tonight. My "Heather Harley" persona is always my most profitable gig. It goes over big with the wealthy, conservative, wanna-be types. Something about the sheer freedom of driving on the open road in high gear, inspires fantasies of that wild, untamable side of them they're all yearning to tap into.

I rummaged through my makeup drawer till I found exactly what I was looking for. I pulled out the long black-feathered earring attached to a silver-winged Harley-Davidson logo and pierced it through my left ear, wearing only a simple cubic zirconia on the other side. I put on a long, dark wig, pinning the hair up with a clip shaped like a silver knife blade and carefully letting a few stray pieces of hair fall provocatively on the nape of my neck. Perfect.

I walked over to my costume rack and put together an outfit that even I had to admit was outrageous. A leather-and-chain G-string was my starting point, and I built my look on that foundation. A black leather-and-lace teddy with garters holding up seamed stockings was next. I covered my curvy hips with a snug, black leather miniskirt and stepped into a pair of four-inch stiletto heels with ankle straps that fastened with little silver Harley-Davidson wings. Damn, I looked hot.

I studied myself in the full-length mirror and had to admit I'd come a long way since my little-girl Catholic-school days. Just the thought of all those years of oppression, both in school and at home, made me shudder. Growing up in my crazy and alcoholic family and being terrorized by a bunch of dysfunctional nuns had made my childhood nothing less than a nightmare. Is it any wonder I never aimed very high in life? The most I was ever encouraged to do was to get married and have babies. The funny thing was, when I looked at how that worked out for my mother, I couldn't see why she would push that same misery on her daughters.

I thought back to a typical day in my unhappy little existence when I was about seven. I came bounding through the back door after school, calling, "Hi, Ma, I'm home," and was quickly told to "hush up" because my father was sleeping. Sleeping it off, was more

85

like it, but even then, I knew better than to say so. That's what my brother, Danny, called it on the mornings after our father would come home in the middle of the night, stumbling and crashing into walls and waking up the whole house. Usually, he just yelled at our mother and called her horrible names, names that I knew I should never repeat. Sometimes, on the really bad nights, he would turn on all the lights and make everyone get out of bed and salute him because he was "king of the castle."

I learned early in life that it was always better to humor my father than to defy him like my big brother, Danny, often did. I watched in horror many a night as Danny and my father duked it out while my mother cowered in the corner with my sister, crying and begging them to stop.

I never got the full brunt of my father's rage, probably because I was the youngest, so I never felt the need to hide with the others. Not that I wasn't terrified, but my hatred was stronger than my fear. No matter how frightened I was, I never allowed myself to cry in front of him. Danny once told me that if you let someone make you cry, you might as well be their slave, and I wasn't about to be a slave to any big, smelly man who terrorized my nights.

It was always a mystery to me that nothing was ever mentioned the next morning at the breakfast table. If anyone dared to bring it up, my mother was quick to remind us that all families had problems and secrets, but that doesn't mean you have to rehash them or, God forbid, tell anyone outside the family about them. She said it was always a better idea to make believe it never happened, especially when my father woke up sick and irritable the next day.

I was always amazed at how willing everyone was to ignore the terror of the night before, though I know now that it was the only way to survive. I may have ignored it along with the rest of them, but I never forgot, and I never even once tried to convince myself it didn't happen.

I remember falling asleep in school some-times after being up all night witnessing one of those scenes. Sister Mary Margaret would make me stand in the back of the room for the whole day, just so I'd stay awake, then send me home with a note for my mother to sign, saying I was "undisciplined" and shouldn't be allowed to watch TV.

That was the year Danny was a high-school senior and my mother was always filling out applications for him to go to college. When I asked why Danny wasn't filling out the appli-cations for himself, she said it was because he wouldn't do a good enough job, since he didn't want to go to college.

Naturally, I asked why he had to go if he didn't want to, but my mother said that boys *have* to go to college because they are the "breadwinners," whatever that meant. When I asked if I could go to college one day, she just laughed and said that all girls have to do is stay pretty and *marry* someone who went to college. I would have stayed and argued with her, but that's when I heard my father come lumbering out of the bedroom, grumbling that dinner wasn't ready yet.

I knew only too well the bedlam that would follow, and I also knew how to shut it out. I ran to my room and flung myself on the bed, wrapping my pillow around my ears and singing my favorite songs as loud as I could, drowning out the insults, the accusations, and the ugly names. Maybe I would never go to college, but I also knew I would never be any man's slave or wife or whatever you wanted to call it. Not ever.

Now I stood looking at myself in a mirror in the back room of a strip joint. I'm all grown up and I answer to no one, and that's just the way I like it. Okay, maybe being a stripper isn't the most respectable profession in the world, but the way I see it, it's a hell of a lot better than what I came from. Maybe someday I'll do better, but for now at least, I'm my own person.

I was startled out of my thoughts by Anthony, the so-called emcee, who always walks into our dressing room unannounced to check out the dancers' look for the night. He stood

89

in the doorway and let out a long, low whistle when he saw me.

"Forget the flattery, Anthony," I said sarcastically, totally annoyed that he took such liberties with our privacy. "Just because you're the owner's son doesn't mean you get anything more than a free look," I went on, purposely avoiding his sex-starved eyes and staring only into the mirror at myself for a final check. "Tell the boys Heather Harley's back in town tonight," I added, plucking a black motorcycle jacket from the rack and brushing past him.

A few minutes later I heard my opening music, "Leader of the Pack," as Anthony announced my number. I sashayed onto the stage and tried to amuse myself by studying the all-male audience as closely as they were studying me.

As usual, the lighting was murky at best and the music was too loud to inspire any type of artistic expression in me. For the fifty-millionth time, I would have to fake it. I reached up to steady myself by keeping one hand on the lowered ceiling, which allows us girls to promenade seductively on the meat rack without losing our balance.

I walked once around the catwalk without revealing anything, just giving the boys something to dream about. Carly Simon is right—"Anticipation" is what it's all about. I studied their pathetic, ravenous expressions as I made my way back to my starting point, where I would begin disrobing, one excruciating layer at a time.

I had just thrown the leather jacket in a heap on one of the tables closest to the stage and was unsnapping the side of my miniskirt when I became aware of a new face among the room full of regulars. He sat alone at a table in the corner, several empty glasses in front of him, and for a moment I felt a wave of sympathy for him, though I don't know why. What was with me lately? Maybe it was because he didn't look like he belonged here; he looked too clean-cut or conservative or something.

The wave of sympathy passed very quickly as I watched him slug down another drink and I was reminded of all the pain alcoholic men have caused in my life. No thanks. I concentrated on my work instead and did some of my best moves, including my infamous "hip twitch," simultaneously peeling off the fingerless, black leather gloves I had donned at the last minute. Maybe it was because of all those childhood memories I'd been exploring earlier that I found myself doing some of my most artistic work in years.

I finished my number with more passion than I'd felt in a very long time, and I must say, my garters were stuffed with money to the point of being uncomfortable. In a way, it was a little embarrassing for my fans to see how much money I made for selling them a fantasy, and I knew I needed to bow out, stash my earnings in a safe place backstage, and then come back out and lure them all into another round.

I did just that. I smiled with my two-thousand-dollar, perfectly capped teeth and winked with just the right amount of feigned intimacy to make every guy in the crowd think it was meant just for him. I learned that trick from an old, pathetic showgirl who had shown up one night and told me she was through with men and that women were much more worthy of relationships and love. I had to agree with her intellectually, yet I knew that on a carnal level I would always find men to be the only gender that attracted me.

So I took my bow, then hurried backstage to count my stash. I was sitting at my dressing table, adding it up, when Anthony knocked and immediately entered, as usual, without waiting for an invitation.

"If you ever wonder why women don't find you attractive," I snarled without looking up from my hoard, "consider the fact that you have the manners of a sex-starved orang-utan."

"You were great, Heather!" Anthony gushed, totally ignoring my insult. "There's at least a zillion guys out there waiting for your next show. We're gonna clean up, babe!"

Anthony calling me "babe" was enough to make me regurgitate the meager dinner I'd eaten earlier, but I knew I needed the calories to get me through my next performance. It just never sat well with me that I did all the work and Anthony and his father made just as much money off my clients as I did . . . for doing nothing. How is it that men have even found a way to capitalize on something that only a beautiful woman can sell? Go figure.

"By the way," Anthony added nonchalantly, "there's some guy who paid me a hundred bucks to come meet you backstage, so don't be surprised when he shows up."

"Get out of here, Anthony," I snapped. "What the hell gives you the right to sell my private time? I better see that whole hundred, you hear me?"

With that, I scraped my chair on the floor as I shoved Anthony through the door of the dressing room and dramatically turned the cheap, malfunctioning lock on its cylinder. I was just touching up my makeup when I heard the unmistakable sound of Anthony's annoying knock on the door again. I took a deep breath, wondering what he wanted now, and I stomped my way over to the door in an attempt to intimidate him.

"You interrupt me one more time and I'm gonna start chargin' *you!*" I bellowed as I swung the door open with all my might and found myself staring at a slightly faded black T-shirt. My eyes immediately traveled upward, taking in every angle and detail on the way up to a lovely and familiar face.

"Joe," I murmured hoarsely. "What are you doing here?" I added, trying to recover from the shock of seeing him here.

"Should I leave?" He laughed, noting my sudden self-consciousness. "I don't know why you're embarrassed to see me under these circumstances," he added. "It's what you normally do, right?"

He was right of course, but for some reason I felt terribly ill at ease, which is most unusual for me. I mean, I'm certainly not ashamed of how I make my living, but it's not exactly the kind of thing I wanted to throw in Joe's face. For some reason, it felt, well, almost sinful, for him to see me like this.

"You know, we really have to talk about this 'sin' thing," he said with an easy grin. "Don't blame me for all that stuff someone wrote in the Baltimore Catechism," he added with an amused chuckle.

There was a musical quality to his laughter that reminded me of the deeper notes on my childhood xylophone. Oddly enough, the pounding music of the band and the clatter of dishes in the kitchen were drowned out by the soothing, lilting resonance of his laugh. Everything seemed to be in slow motion as I watched the smile on his lips slowly spread to his eyes, and I was momentarily captivated by his charm. Those soft brown eyes cast a gentle warmth on me, like a fading summer sun, and once again melted the frozen tundra of my heart.

"I love that you enjoy your sensuality, Heather," he said earnestly. "There's no reason for you to feel uncomfortable with it just because I'm standing here."

"There's not?" I asked, a bit stunned at his response.

"Not at all." He smiled. "I gave it to you to enjoy. It's my gift to you."

I waited for the "but" that I knew was coming, and I wasn't disappointed.

"But," he continued, "your sensuality is only one of many gifts you have. I'd like to see you explore some of the others. I'm sure they would bring you great joy too."

"I must admit, I do have quite a few talents," I admitted honestly, "but this one pays the best."

"You have no idea what great things you're capable of." He smiled again. "Listen, you want to get out of here for a while? Go for a ride maybe?" he asked, changing the subject abruptly. "I'm on my Harley, but you look like you can handle it," he said, studying my Harley-girl costume.

"Yeah, sure," I said, coming out of my trance. "That sounds like a good idea. I just have to freshen up a bit and let Anthony know I won't be back for a second act." I was still trying to collect myself in the face of Joe's overpowering charm, and concentrating on details was the only way I knew to get back to the present moment. "Besides," I added, "he and his father already made a fortune off of me tonight.''

A quirky little smile spread across Joe's lips at that, and I had no idea why. "I'll meet you in the parking lot," he said, then turned on his booted heel and disappeared through the adjacent exit.

6

*I*SLEPT LATE THE NEXT
morning, dreaming of gentle caresses on my
face from some vague and mysterious presence. When I was only partially awake, yet too
close to consciousness to be able to force myself back into that lovely dream state, I opened
my eyes only to discover the soft morning
breeze gently billowing the white chiffon cur-
tains across my face. I smiled in spite of
myself and stretched luxuriously against the
pillows, remembering the night before.

Joe had waited outside the club for me while I informed Anthony that I wouldn't be doing a second show tonight. I locked him out of the dressing room by pushing a chest of drawers against the door and changed into jeans and a light sweater while he stood outside threatening to fire me.

Again I noticed that sensation of incredible lightness as I bounced down the back stairs toward Joe and his waiting Harley. I jumped on and we blasted off into the anonymity of the night, riding fast and riding as one. I had no idea where we were headed, and I didn't care. All I knew was that I was free, at least for now, and that I was determined to have more of these moments.

I yawned and turned over in bed, reenacting in my mind the glorious ride we'd taken along the Pacific Coast Highway and on little-known trails in some of the back canyons. The moon was my favorite kind, the kind I call a "finger-nail moon," when only a tiny sliver lights up a corner of the vast blackness of night. In a way, I felt that's exactly what Joe's presence in my life was doing now, lighting up a little corner of hope in my heart.

We hardly spoke at all, but there was no doubt that we were communicating without words. I'd never experienced anything like that in my life, and I was amazed at the depth of peacefulness I felt. We must have ridden through most of LA's beachfront, then out to the desert in Riverside. The mountains and desert and star-studded sky were exquisitely beautiful, and I got the feeling Joe was wordlessly trying to show me all of the jewels he had laid before us. Jewels that go largely unnoticed.

He dropped me off at my door shortly before midnight and reminded me of our beach plans for the next day. He did that thing again where he kissed his forefinger, then laid it softly on my lips, and he was gone before I even stepped inside the door.

I glanced at my bedside clock and gasped when I realized it was already eleven AM. I rolled out of bed and lumbered into the shower, blaming my exaggerated somnolence on jet lag. I'd have to hurry if I wanted a cup of coffee before Joe picked me up at noon.

At the stroke of twelve, I heard the unmistakable roar of his Harley's engine beneath my kitchen window. "Are you always this prompt?" I called through the screen. He just laughed and revved the engine to hurry me along.

I threw two beach towels into my canvas bag and headed out the door. Climbing on behind him, I took the helmet he handed me and fastened it securely, though I wondered why I should need a helmet with Joe in control of things.

"It sets a good example," he called back to me.

I just smiled and secured my canvas bag to the bar behind me.

"Hungry?" he called over the engine's roar.

"Starving!" I shouted back.

"Good. I know a great spot for lunch; then we'll go to the beach. I hope you're wearing your bathing suit under your clothes," he yelled. "The water's great!"

102

"Well, you can swim," I retorted, "but I'm not going in that freezing cold toilet bowl of an ocean."

"We'll see," was all he said, popping the clutch as our heads jerked back together and we sped off into the splendid summer day.

We drove to a favorite restaurant of mine near Marina del Rey and had lunch outside on the patio. We lingered over our meal, sometimes teasing and laughing and other times engrossed in serious conversation. Eventually we made our way to the beach, where we could watch the fishing boats come in with the day's catch. We walked on the beach and waved to the incoming boats for a long time. We talked to some of the fishermen when they docked, and they showed us what they had caught. Who knew fishermen could be so friendly? Everyone just seemed so at ease with Joe, even though he was a total stranger to them.

It was late afternoon by the time I spread out the beach towels and we settled down on them. The beach was fairly empty now except for a few die-hard sunbathers trying to soak up every last ray of ultraviolet before the sun dipped below the horizon.

We sat there for a few minutes without speaking, just watching the seagulls play and the waves roll in. The sun was beginning to get that late-day orange glow to it, making the beach look almost magical, and I noticed a strange feeling of contentment settle over me.

"I'm glad to see you looking so relaxed," Joe said, putting his hand on my knee and patting it.

"I'm glad to see you're the kind of guy who can sit still on the beach," I answered dryly, "and not feel compelled to throw a football or run after a Frisbee."

He laughed at that, a lovely, resonant laugh that sounded better than any music I've ever heard. I couldn't take my eyes off him, lying there in the sun, dark glasses reflecting my own image staring at him. God, he was so beautiful at that moment, so perfect.

"Believe me, I have my flaws," he warned me, once again reading my thoughts.

"Where? Show me just one," I challenged with utter confidence.

He looked amused at first, then his voice took on a more somber tone. "You didn't think I was so perfect the first time you saw me," he said, smirking. "If I remember correctly, you thought I should be working out and sculpting my body into a work of art."

"That was before I really got to know you," I protested. But he was right. How could I have been so blind, so shallow?

He looked out at the horizon and maybe even further. I noticed the tide was coming in and we were awfully close to the water's edge, yet he had made no attempt to remove his ever-present sneakers or to roll up his jeans.

"I thought you were going for a swim," I said, thinking it odd that he would let his expensive pair of Nikes get wet. He didn't answer with words, but a slow smile crossed his lips.

The ocean waves lapped at his feet and I didn't blame them. If I were an ocean wave, I'd lap at his feet too. The man was not only

105

magnetic and charming, he was obviously far more complex than any man I'd ever met. I mean, I thought I knew men, being in my line of work and all, but Joe, he was, I don't know, *special.*

"Look, Heather, there's something I should tell you," he said, turning his tanned face to me just as the sun pointed its soft, orange spotlight on him.

"Oh, please don't be gay," I said, squeezing my eyes closed and bracing myself.

I heard him laugh, and words cannot describe my relief. I mean, I know you're not supposed to be thinking about physical longings around some guy who just so happens to be God, but I guess I'm not that highly evolved yet. Besides, the only reason those kinds of thoughts even crossed my mind was because I knew it was safe. I knew that Joe would never let that sort of thing happen, and that was part of his charm, I suppose. Joe was the only man I'd ever spent this much time with who hadn't tried to put any moves on me. It's the old story. You always want what you think you can't have. Go figure.

Just then I had a sweeping revelation. None of that stuff really mattered anyway. Joe was more of a man than anyone I'd ever met. I saw a whole man before me, and I loved what I saw, who he was, and that was enough.

Joe sat up then and removed his T-shirt in that masculine way that men do, crossing his arms behind his head and pulling it off in one smooth movement. He tossed the shirt aside, and I sat there spellbound. I assumed he didn't swim in jeans and sneakers, so I waited for them to come off next, but he hesitated.

"What, Joe?" I murmured. "What were you going to tell me?"

"I don't want to shock you," he said gently, locking eyes with me.

"So get it over with," I urged. "The suspense is killing me."

There was a long silence after that. I refused to work any harder for this information. If he wanted to share his secret with me, he was going to have to be brave and go the rest of the way alone. I wasn't going to pull it out of him. I turned my attention instead to the last of the incoming fishing boats as greedy seagulls trailed behind them, screeching, fighting, and announcing their arrival.

"I lost my leg in a boating accident ten years ago," he said somberly.

That got my attention.

"I didn't want to tell you right away," he added, eyes focused on the gold-lamé California sunset. "Somehow it always seems to make people pity me, no matter how good their intentions are. And then they never look at me again without focusing on my loss."

"But you're God," I said. "Just fix it."

"It doesn't work that way," was all he said, and somehow I knew he didn't want to talk about it anymore.

I said nothing because my eyes were glued to his long legs stretched out on the damp sand before him. So *that's* why he hadn't removed those high-top sneakers, no matter how close we got to the water's edge. You don't have to hit me over the head with a brick.

I've never been the shy type, but for perhaps the first time in my life, I felt a little bashful.

Timidly, I stared into his eyes and reached for the leg closest to me. I put my hand on his left knee, and there I felt the hard edge of some kind of contraption that ran the length of what should have been his leg.

I was not about to break the eye contact, but I was also not going to sit there dumbstruck. I reached down and untied the shoelace, then gently, blindly removed the sneaker and the soft woolen athletic sock beneath it. Only then did I break the eye lock to glance down at what he now used for a foot.

It was just a piece of flesh-colored plastic, not grotesque, not repulsive, not anything really. "I want to see the whole thing," I said, suddenly flooded with nerve. "You have your bathing suit on under there, don't you?" I asked. "Let's go swimming."

I saw the hesitation in his eyes, but it passed quickly, and he pulled off his jeans while I discarded my shorts and shirt as well. There we sat, me in a jade-colored one-piece bathing suit and him in a pair of aqua surfer trunks. My eyes went immediately to the prosthesis that started at his knee and did a poor imitation of a warm, living limb.

I placed my hand on the lifeless, cold plastic and surprised even myself with what I said next. "Take it off," I whispered.

He looked at me tenuously. "Are you sure?"

"Do it," I said in a tone not unlike the ones I'd heard many a night from men who watched me dance.

"Heather, are you sure you really want to see this? I don't want to gross you out."

"It's *you*," I answered fervently. "I want to know everything about you."

"It's not a pretty sight, I'm warning you," he tried one last time.

Slowly, very slowly his hand moved down to the rim of the appliance. He kept his eyes glued to my face, searching for just the slightest hint of revulsion. If he saw any sign of it, he would stop, I was certain. He tugged the prosthesis all the way off and placed it on the sand beside him.

What I saw was nothing more than a normal-looking knee with a shin that narrowed into a soft, fleshy, conical end that fit perfectly into the artificial leg he had just removed. There was nothing repulsive about it. It was Joe and I loved him. It was no different from looking at my own elbow if I held my fist to my chin and looked down.

The seagulls flew overhead, swirling above us and chattering endlessly. The sun dropped quickly below the horizon, leaving only a faded wash of pink across the western sky. I sat quietly, studying Joe's old wound, deeply touched by the fact that he had allowed me to see his vulnerability. I didn't remember any man ever letting me get this close to the things that had hurt him.

I noticed the long, raised pieces of scar tissue that ran along the curve of the amputation.

"Those scars," he noted hoarsely, "they're from all the surgery I've had to make it fit better inside my prosthesis. They call them 'stump revisions.' "

I was appalled at the bluntness of the term. "You'd think with all the high-tech phrases these medical people are famous for using, they'd come up with a better name than 'stump revision,'" I said. "Something less archaic, you know?"

"Like what?" He laughed.

"I don't know," I pondered, "but there must be a more poetic way of saying it."

"Yeah, well, next time you run into a trauma surgeon who moonlights as a poet, let me know." He laughed again.

I loved that he could find humor in it, and all I wanted to do was soothe him and hold him and tell him how sorry I was. How could a person as inflexible and shallow as me have made such a radical personality change? I mean, I'd always stood firm in my decision not to accept anything less than physical perfection in men and never to feel sorry for them. Now, here I was falling in love with an amputee. What was happening here?

Wordlessly, Joe began to put the prosthesis back on, but I immediately brushed his hand away saying, "No, not yet."

I'm not exactly sure what came over me, but some unfamiliar emotion welled up from the depths of my heart, and I cradled his stump in my hands, studying the old scars at close range this time. This wasn't pity or sympathy; it was just a sudden comprehension of the pain he'd suffered and an appreciation of the courage it had taken for him to let me in like this. I brought two of my fingers to my lips, kissed them softly, then placed my fingertips on the end of his stump. He made a sound that seemed to come from some deep, unnamed place in his very soul, and I wasn't sure what it meant.

When I looked up, Joe's eyes were glistening with tears, and I was amazed that even God himself would be so moved by such a simple gesture.

"There was nothing simple about that gesture," he murmured softly. "Love like that is what I've been talking about all along. Love like that could heal the world."

I didn't know what to say. It still astounded me to have God's approval for anything, and I simply didn't know how to handle it. "Let's go swimming," I suggested, totally inappropriately.

Joe looked lovingly at me and tugged his prosthesis back on. "You'll have to put this back on the towel for me after I get in the water, okay?" He grinned. "I don't swim with it on."

"Whatever," I called, running ahead of him and diving into the salty splendor of a newly cresting ocean wave.

Joe stood at the water's edge for a moment and watched me bodysurf right up to his feet. I hadn't been in the ocean in years, and I'd forgotten how truly magnificent it felt. I stood up then and walked the few yards to where our towels lay, just as a middle-aged woman passed Joe and smiled at him.

"Toss it here," I called without thinking.

Joe got a mischievous look in his eye, then reached down and pulled off the artificial limb, pitching it right past the startled woman and into my waiting hands. I caught it flawlessly in midair and laid it reverently on my towel, then hightailed it back to the water's edge.

Joe was balancing on one leg, waiting for

me. I suppose he could have hopped easily enough into the water without me, but I was glad he hadn't.

I walked up beside him, and for possibly the first time in my life, I uttered the words, "Here, you can lean on me."

7

*J*OE AND I HADN'T EVEN stayed out late the night before, but I called in sick the next day anyway. I just didn't feel like going to work in that place anymore. At least not today.

I'd made plans for a picnic lunch with Joe for the afternoon, and when he asked what time I'd have to be back to get to work, I told him that I wasn't going in today. He didn't ask why, or how I thought I was going to pay the bills; he simply smiled that charming grin of his and said, "Pick you up at noon."

Not surprisingly, at twelve on the dot, Joe was outside my door on his Harley. He handed me a helmet, then took the picnic basket from my hands and secured it to the back of the bike. We took off with a thunderous roar, and I was certain for a moment that I had died and gone to heaven. Being with Joe just seemed to have that effect on me.

We rode up the coast to a little woodsy canyon buried between the Santa Monica Mountains. I'm not sure if the day was really as perfect as it seemed, or if everything just always had a certain ambience every time I was with Joe. All I know is that the sun shed a gentle warmth on us and the sky looked so clear and so vast, I almost wanted to get swallowed up in it.

We found a small clearing in the woods and spread a blanket on the soft grass, chatting and laughing easily as we opened the picnic basket and dug into the goodies I had packed. We talked about all kinds of things, things I rarely ever thought about, but when the subject came around to the purpose of Joe's presence in my life right now, I got a little nervous.

"No need to be nervous," he said. "I'm only here to help. You know, to teach you the principles you have to master to make yourself happy and fulfilled."

"That's not what scares me," I said through a mouth full of coleslaw.

"Oh?" he said. "What's making you nervous, then?"

"The thought of you leaving me and moving on to the next person, like you told me you would." I heard the tremor in my voice, and I didn't want to cry. I couldn't believe that the thought of a man leaving me could still make me cry. You'd think I'd be used to that by this stage in life.

"Oh, that," Joe said, munching on a potato chip. "Well, there are a lot of people on the planet who need my help. Besides, I never leave any of you. I just kind of fade into the background and guide you from another dimension is all. You've got nothing to worry about."

I understood what he was saying, but I live in *this* dimension, and I wasn't sure I could handle not having Joe around in it to keep me company. He was so good for me. Life is very hard and I needed Joe to keep pointing out the lessons and to keep me on track.

"By the time I'm done with you," he said, grinning, "you'll be able to do a fine job on your own with all that stuff."

"But I can't seem to put certain things behind me, Joe," I said, and a deep anguish surfaced in my voice. It both surprised and embarrassed me.

"Like what?" he asked patiently, the way a compassionate teacher might speak to a frightened child.

"The past, my childhood," I answered, my eyes suddenly downcast, in an unusual moment of self-consciousness. "I mean, I know all that craziness was a long time ago and no matter how awful it was, it's in the past. I know I should be able to move beyond it, but sometimes I just can't."

"It's not always easy to forget, Heather." His words were kind and understanding, and my heart devoured them like warm French pastries wrapped around a sweet and creamy filling. I had expected him to tell me to get tough and to move beyond the pain, and instead, he was sympathizing and supporting me.

I was astonished to feel a big, salty tear slide off my face and splatter onto the ground. How could I be crying? I *never* cried. The only emotion I'd ever had trouble controlling was laughter. But tears? They'd never been a problem for me.

"They've been a bigger problem than you know, perhaps," Joe was saying from somewhere close to my ear. "Tears are as legitimate as laughter, Heather. You must acknowledge them or you lose a part of yourself." He was silent for a moment; then, looking down at his left leg, he added, "And I know what it's like to lose a part of yourself."

I looked over at his artificial left leg, completely camouflaged by jeans and the ever-present high-top sneaker. "What?" I asked, suddenly intrigued by what it was like to be missing a big chunk of yourself. "What's it like to not have your leg? Do you still miss it sometimes or do you somehow get used to it not being there?"

"You get used to everything," he said with a sigh and a knowing grin, "even a traumatic childhood."

"Yeah, I guess," I said, putting my chin in my hand.

"Of course, the pain of an amputation doesn't necessarily go away," he added. "You just get better at dealing with it."

"You mean you still have physical pain from the amputation?" I asked, incredulous that anyone had to endure pain for so many years after the initial trauma.

He put his long fingers beneath my chin and tilted my face like a TV antenna to receive the wisdom that emanated from his eyes. "Didn't you just tell me you still have pain from your childhood," he asked, "even though it isn't there anymore?"

Okay. So there it was. Joe was obviously teaching me another lesson and I hadn't seen it coming.

"Yeah, but that's not the same as physical

pain, the kind you feel when they cut your leg off,'' I insisted. "Is it?" I asked, considering that he just might have a point.

He didn't answer right away, and it seemed to me that an eerie silence fell over the woods. I didn't hear any birds chirping or squirrels jumping from tree branches or even the annoying buzz of flies. Someone once told me that the first sign of an impending earthquake is when all the little forest animals and birds get still like that. Animals are supposedly the first to sense the rumblings of the earth, and suddenly I found myself scanning the area, looking for a place to hide from falling trees.

"The medical profession calls it 'phantom pain,' " Joe continued softly, unconcerned with minor annoyances like earthquakes and completely ignoring the panic in my face. "They have a hard time understanding how something that isn't there anymore can still hurt, but you and me, well, we know. Anything that suddenly gets cut off, whether it's your arm or your leg . . . or your childhood, always leaves a memory of pain."

Phantom pain. What an interesting phenomenon. I'd heard of it before, but I'd never thought about it in terms of my past.

"You see, Heather," he went on, "it's okay for you to cry those tears you've been holding in all these years. Your pain is real, just like the pain in my amputated leg. It's so real, in fact, that sometimes I feel like my left leg is twisted under me and the only thing that helps is for someone to try to position it for me. I know the leg's not really there anymore, but don't try telling that to certain parts of my brain, because that leg will always be a part of me, no matter what."

I was fascinated by what he had said and the way he applied it to me. I felt an incredible sense of relief to know that I wasn't crazy or morbid simply because I couldn't completely forget those old childhood wounds. But what now? Did this mean that none of us can ever rise above the traumas of our lives? I certainly didn't relish the idea of being an eternal victim of my childhood.

Joe's soft touch on my shoulder brought me out of my thoughts, and when I met his gaze, it was as though he were shooting darts of love into my very soul. And he hit a bull's-eye every time.

"Love yourself, Heather," he said, smiling. "Love everything that is you. You're not damaged by anything if you learn the lesson that's wrapped inside. Remember that."

"The lesson," I repeated slowly as I tried to process the information. I desperately wanted to make sure I understood everything he was teaching me. "So how do you deal with the loss of your leg?" I urged him. "Can any lesson really be worth that price?"

"This one was." He grinned, tapping the hollow plastic that was now his leg. "The lesson was that we are not our bodies. Our bodies are simply a container for who we really are."

I was impressed. And embarrassed. Once again I was reminded of how shallow my constant quest to perfect my own body was and how silly I'd been demanding nothing less from the men in my life. No wonder I never seemed to find meaningful relationships.

"What about me, Joe?" I asked earnestly.

"What was the point of growing up in an alcoholic, dysfunctional home? Where's the lesson in that?"

"You mean you haven't figured that out yet?" he asked with a teasing glint in the soft brown eyes. "Are you going to make me spoon-feed you everything?"

I didn't laugh. This was too important and I wanted to get it right. "C'mon," I said, pouting, "tell me."

"Okay." He smiled. "You've worked pretty hard so far. I suppose you've earned a freebie." Then he looked around at the leaves rustling in the late-summer breeze and the colony of ants that were climbing the trunk of the tree we leaned on. "Don't panic on me again and go thinking we're going to have an earthquake," he said as every living thing he rested his eyes upon stopped in its tracks, including the breeze and the ripples in the nearby pond. I stared at the silent scene speechlessly for a moment, then looked up at Joe, who shrugged his broad shoulders and grinned. "It helps with your concentration," he explained. "This is a really important lesson for you, Heather, and I don't want any distractions, okay? Ready?"

I was more than ready, so I closed my eyes and tried to concentrate on being receptive to what he was about to teach me. I wanted to know what all that childhood pain and the struggles with my self-esteem had really been about. What purpose could it possibly have served?

"Open your eyes," he prodded gently. "I want to look in there and speak directly to your heart."

I obeyed, and suddenly he concentrated all of his energy into his eyes, then poured it out gently, knowingly into mine, like a mother bird skillfully placing a freshly caught worm into the open and hungry mouth of her young.

"History is not irreversible," he said, as his eyes held me captive. "It never matters what you come from," he went on. "You can always change paths and find the light in your own life."

I swallowed hard, past the lump of tears in my throat that threatened to burst into a never-ending river, spilling the relief I felt all over the forest floor. "You mean I don't have to end up doing this stripping gig forever?" I asked tearfully, shocked that I could finally admit to myself . . . and to Joe, how much I detested it.

Joe's eyes took on an almost glazed look as he held me spellbound with a magnetic-like power. I suddenly realized that there was no ceiling or floor to the depth in those engulfing brown eyes; there was only an endlessness to everything he said and thought.

Carefully, he lifted his hand and placed two fingers lovingly over my lips, simultaneously quieting my mouth and my mind. *"Shhhhh. Do you hear something?"* he asked.

I didn't hear a thing and was quick to say so. In fact, I didn't want anything to interrupt this very personal and maybe even life-changing insight I was having with Joe.

Then I heard it too. The sound was riveting and unmistakable. Somewhere, close enough to be heard, was a wailing infant.

But wait a minute, what was a crying baby doing out here in the middle of nowhere? In the middle of the woods? Where were its parents and what kind of a parent would bring such a young child into the middle of this insect-infested environment?

Wherever the child was, the wails of the infant grew louder, and I looked at Joe with a question in my eyes instead of in my mouth for once.

"We have to find it," Joe said calmly. "It sounds like the cries are coming from over there," he added, pointing behind me.

We rose in unison, and suddenly I didn't feel resentful anymore. After all, it was only an innocent baby that was interrupting us. How could I possibly resent the needs of a helpless infant intruding on my time with Joe?

Some kind of uncanny radar welled up in me and I knew *exactly* where to find the child. I knew even before Joe did, and I led the way, knowing that I would eventually need to figure out how I could possibly know something before Joe did, but that wasn't important at the moment. The child's cry was clearly one of distress, and finding that poor helpless little thing in this unforgiving environment was the priority. There would be plenty of time later to discuss this inner knowing with Joe.

I followed the cries and brushed away a large branch of something thorny and green in order to find the child. It scratched my skin, leaving a long, red streak along the inside of my arm, and for once in my life I didn't care what I looked like or what kind of damage was being done to my well-cared-for alabaster skin.

Like a mad woman, I moved another thorny branch out of my way and then another until, finally, I stood before the sight of a newborn baby wrapped in a pink blanket, nestled in a bed of dried twigs and soft green leaves. I didn't need the soft pink cloth to tell me that she was a girl. I instinctively knew that. There was a gentleness and an unmistakable femininity about her that could not be denied.

Instantly, I felt an overpowering affection for this tiny bundle of life, and I plucked her from the ground, clutching her to my heart as though I'd been searching for her for a very long time. Somehow I just knew that more than anything else in the world, she needed me. Not just anyone, she needed *me*. Part of me was surprised at the instant connection and devotion I felt for her, and part of me wasn't surprised at all.

She stopped crying the moment I picked her up, as though she recognized that now she was exactly where she belonged. I rocked her gently, and my arms felt as though they had suddenly discovered the only reason for their existence. I closed my eyes and breathed in the sweet, innocent smell of her, and I would have to say that nothing else in the universe mattered at that moment.

Even the fine mist of sweat that glistened on her smooth forehead smelled sweet and perfect. I thought about all the artificial scents I had been drawn to over a lifetime, the aroma of candles, perfume, and potpourri, and now I realized that, finally, here was a fragrance that could never be imitated. This was something real; something lovely and unique. Thankfully, authenticity is impossible to duplicate.

"Hold her close," I heard Joe say from somewhere near me. "Hold her close, Heather, and never let her go."

I closed my eyes and did exactly as he said. I kissed the soft, innocent skin of her fuzzy little head, and I knew an ecstasy that I was certain no one before me had ever known. "Who are you?" I whispered into her perfect little ear. "Who left you alone out here like this?"

"Don't you know?" Joe asked softly from behind me.

I turned to him, my eyes wide with unanswered questions. "Who?" I begged. "Who would do this to such a helpless little thing?"

He said nothing as he reached out to smooth the blond peach fuzz on her enticingly soft head, and she gurgled with contentment.

"Joe, tell me," I urged. "You're supposed to know these things. Who is she?"

Again my question was answered with nothing but knowing silence.

I looked down at the tiny, warm bundle

cradled in my arms, and now I was overcome with a feeling of familiarity, of some long-ago link between us.

"Oh, my God," was all I could manage to say.

"That's right, Heather," Joe said reassuringly. "She's you."

I knew it. Even before he'd said it, somehow I had known it. I recognized her. She was sweet and vulnerable, and for whatever reason, things had gone terribly wrong in her life already. No one had protected her. No one had nurtured her or kept her safe. She hadn't had a chance to be the dependent little being she was meant to be for now.

I was aware of Joe's presence, yet, in some sense, there was no one else in the world at that moment except this helpless baby and me. And we were one.

I studied every detail of her being and swallowed her with my eyes. I marveled at the unlined skin, the flawless, miniature body, and the clean slate of a mind that knew no self-consciousness. I thought about how babies don't look funny without teeth or hair.

Instead, they just look perfect. They demand
your attention by being purely what they are.
Unlike most adults, they have no pretenses
and they make no effort to impress, to com-
pete, or to stand out.

Tiny, uncoordinated fingers tangled in a
loose strand of my hair, and her little pink
mouth opened simultaneously. In a moment
that passed far too quickly, she smiled the
quivering, spellbinding grin of an infant, and
I have never known a more pure joy than what
I felt at that moment.

As if from a far-off cave, I heard the echo of
Joe's voice. "That's right, Heather. Love her.
It's about time. She's . . . You've . . . needed
this for a very long time. You've both been
hurt. Embrace her. Love her. She is a little
being who didn't get what she needed all
those years ago. Give it to her now. Heal her."

It was at that precise moment I was truly
convinced this innocent baby and I were the
same person. I loved her and I had an overwhelming urge to protect her . . . to be all
things to her.

I looked into the endless depths of the slate

blue eyes of a newborn, and in them I glimpsed the edge of a completely different world from the one in which I live. It was a world that held me captive with its sheer openness, boundless love, and untapped potential. I saw the seeds of a whole lifetime in those eyes, and I wanted desperately to protect, support, and nurture that fragile little bud of humanity.

Tears of rapture streamed down my face and fell onto her delicate, pink cheek, and I knew that something in me was finished now. Completed. Healed. I wondered how this tiny, helpless bundle could have such power over me, but I was glad that she did.

"You see, Heather," I heard Joe murmur in my ear, "you've healed both your wounds, and you've brought each other back to life."

"Now what?" I whispered, closing my eyes.

"Hold her close," he instructed. "Hold her as close to your heart as you possibly can."

I kissed the top of her head and lifted her to my heart. She nestled her head against my chest, molding her perfect little body to the contours of my own. I felt butterfly puffs of breath against my skin, puffs of angel breath, and you could never have convinced me that there wasn't the essence of an angel within her tiny form. She was everything that was beautiful, hopeful, and real in the world, and I knew that no matter where life led her, there would always be this perfect presence within her, no matter how deeply it got buried. I felt her melting into me as we became one, and it was the most hypnotic, most fulfilling experience of my life.

135

"Good. That's very good," I heard Joe say lovingly. "Hold her, Heather, and love her. Just like that. Oh, yes, that's very good."

There was silence for a long time as I reached back over twenty-nine years of measured time and loved this little life force that once was me. I nuzzled her, breathed in her fading essence, engulfed her with my heart, and when I eventually opened my eyes, my arms were empty and I searched Joe's waiting gaze for an explanation.

"What happened?" I asked, somewhat dumbfounded. "Where did she go?"

"She's inside of you now," Joe answered

quietly. "Right where she belongs. Love her and always take care of her because she will never stop needing you."

Tears spilled from some old, wounded part of me and trickled off my chin. "I know what I have to do now," I sobbed. "It's time to start taking very good care of myself. Time to cherish the real Heather Hurley . . . whoever *that* is," I sniffled.

Joe handed me a spotless white handkerchief. "I assure you," he whispered earnestly, "Heather Hurley is a wonderful human being."

With that, he reached for my hand and led me silently out of the forest.

8

IN THE DAYS THAT FOL-
lowed, I forced myself to continue working at
the club, though it had become a huge burden
of late. The conversations I had with Joe made
things very clear to me, and I knew it was
just a matter of time before I would have to
be true to myself and find a better way to
make a living. A way that didn't dilute my
very soul.

I would be eternally grateful to Joe for all
the wisdom he imparted to me, but I won-

dered why we had never really discussed his amputated leg again and why he hadn't just magically fixed everything for himself. He had aspirations of accomplishing great things here on earth, helping people to help themselves. Why would he willingly choose to challenge himself with an amputation? Wasn't life hard enough?

We were sitting out on my patio one evening, enjoying the late-summer breeze that wafted softly across our faces and rustled the leaves on my tomato plants. "So, if you really are God, or whatever it is you call yourself these days," I challenged, "why don't you just 'heal thyself'?"

I mean, really, what was the point in walking around minus a leg if you really didn't have to? If I were God, I certainly wouldn't let anything impair me. I definitely don't like to suffer, and I couldn't help but wonder why all these religious types seem to think there's some kind of glory in suffering. That's something I never really understood.

"Because it wouldn't be fair," Joe answered

matter-of-factly. "It may be hard to believe," he continued, "but the funny thing is that everyone here on earth has the same amount of troubles. I went to great pains to make sure no one person had any more or any less heartache in their life than everyone else. The thing I didn't count on was the vast difference in the capacity of each human being to handle sorrow." He said it almost wistfully, as though he was genuinely impressed with the human race. I wasn't going to argue with him there.

"Some people are just so great," he went on. "You throw them a curve ball and they just handle it and say 'Okay, what else have you got up your sleeve for me?' I mean, they not only find a way to cope with it, but they're poised and ready for whatever is next . . . and they take the gift that's wrapped inside and keep moving forward." He looked pensive for a moment then, and added, "Even *I* never knew people could be so resilient. Especially women. I had no idea what incredible beings I had created in them."

I could have told him that.

A few moments elapsed before he spoke again, and I felt no obligation to fill the silence. This was definitely his show, and I wasn't about to interfere.

"Of course, there are always the ones who complain about every little ache and pain and inconvenience in their lives," he said blandly, "but they're the ones who really suffer, because they can't see the incredible gifts I've given them. They seem almost afraid to believe that life can be good, that the hard stuff is just as much of a gift as the easy stuff. They don't seem to appreciate the handcrafted lessons in the middle of the problems, lessons that were meant to make their lives easier and easier."

"Well, you still haven't explained why you didn't just grow another leg," I insisted.

"Haven't I?" he asked, dark eyes glowing like embers that were fanned from some very deep place inside of him. "I thought you understood that, Heather." There was something about the way he said my name that made me feel like a sixties teenager at a Beatles concert.

"Maybe I missed it," I conceded. "But isn't life tough enough without having to use a prosthesis? Why don't you just grow a new leg and get on with your mission here?" I asked, certain that I was making perfect sense.

He stared long and hard at me, not in a judgmental way, but in a deep and probing way. "It wouldn't be fair," he finally repeated. "I didn't put anyone here without some kind of challenge in their lives," he continued. "What would be the point?" He didn't wait for me to answer before adding, "Besides, how could I give everyone an equal share of problems and then not give myself any at all? Really, Heather, what kind of guy do you think I am?"

I had no idea how to answer that question; I only knew I wished there were more like him. I was intrigued by what he was saying. "Are you trying to tell me that babies born with birth defects and princesses and stockbrokers on Wall Street and people born in third-world countries and doctors and cops and maybe even strippers, all have the same amount of stress and pain in their lives? The same amount of unhappiness?"

"That's exactly what I'm saying," he replied with utter and unquestionable sincerity. "You can't even imagine what lengths I went to in order to be certain that no one got short-changed in the process. The only difference among people is the way they handle their challenges. Some don't even bat an eye, while others cry and complain all the way through life."

"Oh," was all I was capable of saying as I looked back on all the complaining I'd done since I'd met him.

He smiled warmly at me, then added, "There's nothing wrong with a little complaining, Heather, as long as you get right to work fixing whatever it is that is causing your pain."

I was honestly overwhelmed with my capacity for loving him at that moment. There seemed to be no limit to it. As always, though he knew everything about me, he never once criticized me. Me! A so-called fallen woman, a heathen . . . a stripper! How could any woman resist falling in love with a man like that?!

But he was God; he should be used to people adoring him and, well, I guess, loving him. What was there not to love? The man knew everything about me, yet never judged me, never tried to change me. For the first time in my life, I understood the story of how Mary Magdalene once washed his feet with her tears and dried them with her long, abundant hair. Of course that was in the days when he'd allowed himself to have two feet.

I had always resented that story, especially as a young child in parochial school. Even at age six, I had found the concept of a woman washing a man's feet degrading to my gender. I always figured it was far better to have them lusting after me. Yet here I was, falling into the incredible depths of Joe's bottomless eyes, suddenly wanting to do whatever it would take to sooth his disappointment in the human race. If Joe's behavior was an example of the kind of compassion we should all show to our fellow humans, I was certain most of us had been doing a pretty shabby job, at best. For the first time in years, I felt a little ashamed.

His warm hand encompassed my shoulder then, and he said simply, "Don't."

" 'Don't' what?" I asked, still unaccustomed to the fact that he could hear my thoughts.

"Don't obsess on the past," he said, tenderly brushing a strand of hair from my face. "You're doing the best you can, and that's all I ask." We were both quiet for a long moment; then he added, "My most precious gift to you is the present moment. Use it to heal the wounded past."

Those were the last words I thought about before falling asleep that night. "Don't obsess on the past. . . . My most precious gift to you is the present moment." The words tumbled softly off my lips like a magical mantra as I relinquished all the meaningless, extraneous thoughts of my consciousness and slipped aimlessly into a soft, vast cocoon of slumber and dreams.

I was languidly aware of the familiar scent of salt-saturated air and the feel of tepid ocean waves, lapping at my bare feet and sending rays of warmth and well-being throughout my entire body. The sun was not the white-hot fireball of mid July, but rather a gentle caress of warmth upon my skin. I breathed in the salty splendor and tilted my face up to absorb all of the sun's loveliness, as earth and sky conspired to fill me with a sense of wholeness and utter contentment.

It was then that I noticed I was holding something flimsy in my hands. For some reason known only to dreamers, I was unable to identify it with my eyes, but whatever it was, I somehow knew it held great power for me.

I examined the fragile parcel with only my hands, noting its small, square shape and slightly craggy texture. I had the urge to hold it to my heart, and as I did, I found myself soaring through the cloudless, wide-open spaces of that boundless summer sky.

Far above the beach and the sea I sailed. I

passed a flock of pelicans gliding gracefully through their celestial playground before dipping down to scoop their next meal from the smorgasbord the ocean waves offered them. I held the square object in my hands at a different angle, and gently my body swerved in the same direction. Whatever the object was, it had given me wings of a sort and it was directing my flight path. As long as I had the mysterious object in my hands, I knew my flight was guided by something much bigger than me. I aimed it upward and went higher still, finding myself among a group of seagulls at play, and I was overwhelmed with the pure joy of being, for once in my life, in harmony with the universe.

I flew even higher, not at all frightened or concerned about how I was going to get down. The higher I went, the better I felt, and suddenly I knew why birds sing for no apparent reason. I sang too, though for the life of me, I can't remember the song. An odd sensation seized me then, something I had never felt before. It was as though someone had opened a secret door to my very soul and begun filling it with a warm, syrupy liquid that gave my entire body a golden glow.

When it seemed my soul had been filled to overflowing, I sensed that I was beginning to float ever-so-gently back down to earth. I drifted listlessly, swaying quietly through the luminous sky. I passed the seagulls on the way down and smiled wordlessly at them. I passed the pelicans next, and a few of them seemed to be showing off for me as they nose-dived into the turquoise ocean waves for their dinner.

I felt my feet touch the sun-warmed sand, and I was content to be back where everything was familiar again. I glanced down at the mysterious package still clutched in my hands and was surprised by what I saw.

It was several blank pages of very expensive looking stationery bound together with a blue velvet ribbon. There was something written in calligraphy across the top of the first page. *"Heather's Hurdles,"* it said, and I felt a question ripple the smooth surface of my placid mind. Before the question completely formed though, a feather, the color of golden sand, floated softly past my face and landed perfectly in the middle of the page, dripping ink and leaving a stain in the shape of a kiss.

I felt a vaguely familiar sensation closing in on me that I recognized as impending consciousness. I didn't want to wake up yet, so I tried to concentrate on the exquisite stationery, the feathered pen, and the sun-drenched sand under my toes. I wasn't ready to lose the dream, not yet. I wanted to know the meaning of that odd little heading on the stationery, to see what magic the feathered pen would spill onto the pages next, and, oh, how I wanted to fly again!

Reluctantly, I woke up, fighting valiantly for just one more moment of that glorious and intriguing dream. But no, I was undeniably planted firmly in my bed, the alarm clock buzzing next to my head, as obnoxious as the buzzers that announce halftime at basketball games.

I lay there for a moment, gathering my thoughts and trying to remember why I had set the alarm in the first place. Oh, that's right. I had an appointment that morning with a personal trainer to work on tightening my abs. I groaned prematurely and, with a reluctant sigh, rose from the snug womb of my bed to face the world head-on.

I padded into the kitchen, eyes like half-closed venetian blinds, driven only by the need for a caffeine jolt. Plugging in the coffee-maker, I nodded good morning to the man sitting at my breakfast table as I reached for the specialty blend sitting on the counter. Halfway through tearing open the foil bag, I gasped, whirling around in terror to face him, scattering freshly ground hazelnut coffee clear across the kitchen floor.

Joe chuckled softly, shaking his head in amusement as he watched me try to calm myself.

"Took you long enough to notice," he teased.

"You just about scared me to death!" I scolded, once I was able to find my voice. I stood there trying to still the thunder in my chest and calm the uproar in my stomach.

"Sorry about that," he apologized. "I guess I thought you'd be used to this kind of thing by now."

"Used to seeing a strange man sitting at my breakfast table?" I shot back. "Oh, silly me, for finding that a bit unnerving!" I noticed a tremor in my voice, and I could tell that he picked up on it as well.

His amused demeanor immediately melted to a compassionate and contrite posture. He said nothing with his mouth, but his eyes transmitted an ocean of sympathy. Gracefully, he rose from his chair and made his way across the coffee-splattered floor where I stood, my back still pressed up against the sink in a defensive stance.

"I'm sorry I frightened you," he murmured, an almost tangible sense of sincerity surrounding him. He placed one protective hand on my elbow and the other beneath my chin, gently tilting my face up to the lure of his magnetic eyes. "It's easy for me to forget how scared you get sometimes," he confessed. "I keep forgetting that you haven't learned that lesson yet."

The tension in my shoulders and back dissolved, and I leaned casually now against the sink, lost in the depths of his face, exquisitely aware of his comforting touch.

"What lesson?" I finally managed to get out. "I should have known there'd be a lesson hidden somewhere in the midst of you giving me heart failure."

"You don't have to be afraid anymore, Heather," he said. "That's the lesson."

What did he mean by that? I wondered. That nothing bad will ever happen again?

That I no longer have to lock my doors and windows because no harm can possibly come to me? I could live with that.

"Hold on a minute." He laughed. "I don't think you've quite got the gist of what I'm saying."

"I knew that sounded too good to be true," I muttered.

"Wait, Heather," he insisted. "You don't have to be afraid anymore because now you know that I am always with you. I am never farther away than your next breath or your next heartbeat. You never really believed that before. Trust me on this," he finished earnestly.

I had no doubt that he believed what he was saying, but I wanted more than the promise of his presence. I wanted guarantees that nothing would ever go wrong again in my life. That nothing would ever hurt me or stress me in any way.

He addressed my concern even before I could put it into words.

152

"Believe me, a life without challenges to conquer would be hell on earth," he said knowingly. "Where there is pain, always, there is growth," he added quietly. "Remember that. And growth is the sole purpose of life."

"This is too heavy for me to absorb this early in the morning." I sighed, exasperated.

He smiled sympathetically and dropped his gaze to the white linoleum floor, now freckled with hazelnut coffee. "I don't suppose you have any more of that coffee left," he mused with the hint of a smile playing on his lips. "It sure smells good."

I glanced down at the bag that now lay at

my feet, its contents spilled across the floor. I looked back up to Joe's waiting eyes and sighed again.

"Where there is pain, there is growth," I announced, deadpan. "We'll have to drink instant."

*J*OE AND I SAT AT MY KITCH-
en table for a long time that morning, sipping
instant coffee and talking about the impor-
tance of being happy with yourself. His in-
sights and revelations were like a cool,
billowing breeze on my overheated mind,
much like the late-summer breeze that rustled softly through the kitchen window.

I poured what had to be at least our third
cup of the substitute coffee and thought it
smelled suspiciously like the gourmet hazel-

nut coffee I had hurled across the room earlier.

"I think I'm hallucinating," I said, giggling. "I'm craving that hazelnut coffee so much, I'm beginning to think I smell it."

Joe said nothing, just raised his cup in the air for a toast with mine, then placed his curvy lips on the rim, his eyes never leaving my face.

I took a sip of the heated, aromatic brew, then began telling Joe about my strange flying dream last night. Halfway through the first sentence though, I halted and looked down into my coffee cup. I could have sworn I tasted the hazelnut coffee instead of the cheap, instant variety. But that was impossible. Wasn't it?

"Chances are," Joe said, grinning devilishly, "if it looks like hazelnut, smells like hazelnut, and tastes like hazelnut, it probably is."

"How did you do that?" I asked, my eyes wide with wonder. Was there no limit to his talents? Would this man ever stop astonishing me?

"If you really want to see astonishment," he all but gloated, "you should have been there when I turned water into wine. Coffee, that's easy. Wine's a lot tougher because you have to make sure you age it just right."

I stared at him mutely, my mouth hanging open.

"Better close your mouth or you'll be catching flies," he quipped, a playful grin on his charming face. "Now, why don't you get back to telling me about your flying dream," he suggested nonchalantly.

156

I hesitated for only a moment, then took a deep breath and began my saga again. I told him all about the wonderful sensation of soaring through the endless sky, leaving all my cares far beneath me. I tried to describe the utter joy and peace I had felt, the absolute freedom and the feeling of oneness with the universe. I described how the small packet of fine stationery had seemed to act as a throttle and that as long as I held it in my hands, I felt I could fly forever.

Joe sat quietly, taking it all in and smiling

encouragement in all the right places. When I finished, I took a long, slow sip of my coffee, inviting the last vestiges of the dream to wash over me again.

"Really, Joe," I added, "if I didn't know better, I'd swear I actually was flying last night."

He stared quietly at me for a moment, locking eyes with me, then earnestly asked, "What makes you think you weren't?"

I searched for the hint of a smile or a tease in his voice, but there was none. He was completely serious. But how could that be? How could he think I was actually outside flying around last night? "Well, I woke up smack in the middle of my bed this morning," I answered a little self-righteously, "exactly where I started out before falling asleep."

"So?"

"No, no, no," I said, shaking my head in disbelief. "Don't do this."

He laughed then and sat back in his chair, his lanky frame suddenly appearing much too large to be comfortable in my cramped little

157

kitchen. "Why not?" he insisted. "Maybe it's time to start opening your mind to broader possibilities in life, Heather."

"Let's sit in the living room," I suggested, gracefully trying to change the subject. I was not ready to even consider that I might have been flying over Santa Monica the night before, clutching a packet of stationery to my chest. That was a bit too much to fathom. I poured us each another cup of coffee and busied myself with putting bagels and cream cheese on a tray. Suddenly I was ravenous.

"It's your mind that's ravenous." Joe smiled knowingly as we retreated to the couch. "You're ravenous for knowledge," he went on, taking a seat beside me. "You're hungry to know how to fly again. You have a craving to understand the meaning of the stationery you were holding in that dream and to interpret the significance of the feathered pen that kissed your paper."

"I don't believe in interpreting dreams," I replied with a tinge of annoyance.

"I see." Joe nodded patiently while he spread a huge gob of cream cheese onto his bagel. "I suppose that's why your life is such a barrel of laughs."

That comment certainly got my Irish up. "Now, wait just a minute!" I argued. "You're the guy who just finished telling me that life's not always supposed to be easy. That challenges and growth are what it's all about! Now you're trying to sell me all this *woo-woo* stuff about interpreting dreams?" I knew I had him cornered and I loved it.

"I didn't mean to imply that life has to be gruesome," he answered calmly. "Learning and growing can be a lot of fun, and dream interpretation can be a powerful tool." He hesitated for only a moment, then added, just loud enough for me to hear, "If you have the right attitude, that is."

159

"And just what is wrong with my attitude?!!" I shot back, both hands on my hips.

His laughter was maddening as he responded, "Oh, nothing. Just a little, well, 'East Coast,' don't you think?"

I sat there dumbfounded, trying to think of a logical and cutting retort, but my mind was blank.

"That's good, Heather," he soothed, rising from the couch and making his way toward the cedar hope chest I keep in the corner of the room. "A blank mind is like an empty vessel that is finally able to receive."

With that, he nonchalantly opened the hope chest and dug to the bottom, as if he knew exactly what he was looking for. I had no idea what was even in that chest anymore. I hadn't seen the inside of it in years, and frankly, I wasn't sure I wanted to see it now.

Apparently I didn't have a choice in the matter. Joe rummaged around in there until his hand fell upon something that brought a slow smile to his lips. Carefully, he lifted it out of the chest and held it up to me, a look of triumph on his lovely face. An eerie feeling washed over me as my eyes fell on the bundle of frayed papers he held . . . tied together with a blue ribbon, just like the one in my dream.

Ordinarily I would have been outraged if anyone, especially a man, were to take such liberties with my privacy. But Joe wasn't just anyone. Somehow I trusted him with even more than my life, I trusted him with my heart. And I hadn't trusted anyone with *that* in a very long time.

"Why don't you tell me about these," he prodded gently, dropping the neat little bundle into my lap.

"I don't even remember what's in here," I admitted, stalling for time, though I strongly suspected it was a collection of the poetry I used to write.

Joe settled down beside me on the sofa and looked over my shoulder as I hesitantly untied the blue ribbon and began leafing through the worn pages. I skimmed through much of it, painfully remembering how I used to wear my heart on my sleeve, embarrassed that I had ever put such personal feelings down on paper. The whole thing made me very uncomfortable, and I simply did not want to look that far back in my life.

I patted the edges of the loose papers back into some kind of disheveled pile and reached for the blue ribbon to secure them again, just as Joe's graceful hand settled on top of mine. "Don't," he said softly. "You can't always tie things up in neat little bundles and hide them away." With great precision, he reached for a sheet from the middle of the pile, holding it up for me to see. "This is my favorite," he said, smiling warmly. "You really got to me with this one."

Hesitantly, I retrieved it from his hand and read the words that had drained from some old, painful wound.

<u>162</u>

Doing Time

The prisoner sat alone in his cell,
Begging his God to end this long hell.
Oh, such a waste, cut down in his prime
Just for committing a small, human
crime.

He yearned to know freedom and
sunshine and flowers,
Have someone to be with to fill up the
hours.
But there was no hope, for his life was
through,
Then onto his window, a sparrow flew.

"Ah, little friend, I envy you so
To be free to choose where your life will
    go."
The sparrow stared blankly, still perched
    on the ledge,
Eyeing the feline beneath in the hedge.

"Ah," said the sparrow, his voice filled
    with grief,
"I may as well be the thief.
For though I am good and committed no
    crime,
We, each in our own way, are all doing
    time."

I remembered writing that poem right after high school graduation. I had been waiting tables at Vinnie's Diner and feeling very trapped, almost like a prisoner in the little one-horse town where I grew up. Everyone looked so boring and bland to me, and I was petrified of becoming just like them one day. That's when I had decided that someday, I didn't know when, but someday, I would pack my meager bags and hightail it for Los Angeles. I was certain LA held a kind of special magic and that I'd at least have a shot at success and glamour out there.

"And what are you feeling now?" Joe was asking tenderly, apparently having heard every thought that floated through my mind. "Is LA everything you wanted it to be?"

"Of course not," I answered a bit impatiently. "Nothing is ever the way you dream about it being when you're a kid. It's only natural to be a little disappointed."

"Is that all you feel?" he persisted. "Just disappointed?"

I was surprised to feel tears spring to my eyes when he asked me that, yet I wasn't at all self-conscious about it. "I guess I still feel a little trapped," I admitted, as the tears spilled over and ran down my face. "I feel *very* trapped, in fact." I was crying full force now. "Just like I did at Vinnie's Diner. Maybe worse."

Joe leaned over to put a strong, comforting arm around me then, accidentally knocking my bagel onto the couch.

"Whoops," he apologized into my ear, brushing crumbs off the cushion with his free hand. "I didn't mean to get crumbs on your nice sofa."

"That's okay," I sniffled, not wanting him to ever take his arm off my shoulders. "There've been bigger crumbs than that on this couch."

We both looked at each other for a moment, then started laughing.

"My sweet Heather," he murmured, composing himself and stroking my hair. "You have no idea how much magic is right inside of you. You've been obsessing about the outside of you for so long that you've overlooked your greatest treasures."

"Oh, here it comes," I said miserably. "I suppose you're going to tell me to go to college, get a degree, *do* something with my life." I braced myself for the lecture I'd already given myself at least a hundred times so far. The one I knew I would never heed.

"College?" Joe repeated, genuinely surprised at where I thought this conversation was going. "Is that really what you thought I was going to say?"

"Why not?" I muttered. "It's probably the most logical thing."

"It's only logical if it suits your heart's desires," Joe replied. "And I suspect your heart's desires have very little to do with anything that can be taught in a college classroom. In fact," he added with an amused grin, "I strongly suspect you could teach most college professors a thing or two."

I looked up at his marvelous face, searching for a hint of sarcasm or double entendre, but all I saw was love emanating from the depths of his dark brown eyes, penetrating the barriers of my very soul. For at least the millionth time, I marveled at the fact that this man so genuinely loved me, warts and all.

"Tell me, Joe," I urged. "What *are* my greatest treasures? Tell me, because I have no idea."

He glanced down at the yellowed pages of poetry in my lap, and his voice was soft as a kiss when he finally spoke. "Your paintings," he said. "You are a woman of many talents, but your paintings are your greatest gift to the world."

"My *paintings?!*" I scowled. "What paintings?" I thought I had been following his train of thought until this point. I had never painted a thing in my life, and I was certain that I was not one of those people who had some undiscovered potential in the arts. What could he possibly be thinking?

"These paintings," he replied matter-of-factly, shuffling through the pages of poetry in my lap. "You've managed to paint some incredible pictures of powerful emotions. That's not easy to do." He gazed up to make sure I hadn't fainted, I suppose. "And you've used only the finest tools," he added.

"Tools?" I asked, dumbstruck.

"Oh, yes," he went on enthusiastically. "You painted these pictures with words and feelings, and most importantly, you used honesty. And I think you know how hard *that* is to find. You, Heather, are a fine artist."

I was terribly confused and did not hesitate to say so. All of these years I had thought of myself as not very smart, maybe even a little lazy, and certainly not talented. Well, at least not in the usual sense of the word. Yet, here was this mystical being, telling me how wonderful my poems were, calling them paintings, and calling me an artist. What could he possibly have up his sleeve? I wondered.

I didn't have to wonder for long.

Joe absently tied the blue ribbon around the sheaf of papers again and handed me the whole package.

"Close your eyes," he instructed, and with nothing but utter trust, I did as I was told. "Now hold your poems close to your heart," he murmured softly. "That's right," he encouraged. "Do you feel it yet?"

"Feel what?" I asked doubtfully, eyes squeezed tightly closed.

"The magic," was all he said.

Then indeed, I felt it.

I was soaring through the sky again, just as I had in my flying dream the night before. I used the sheaf of papers as a throttle again, and sure enough, it worked. As long as I kept my poetry close to my heart, I could steer myself in any direction I wanted to go. It was a glorious feeling, and I reveled in it for several intoxicating moments.

"I'm flying, Joe!" I cried. "I'm flying again!"

"I know," I heard him say from somewhere down on earth. "I'm proud of you."

He was proud of me? Someone was actually proud of me? It was a splendid feeling, and I never wanted it to end. In my enthusiasm to understand what it all meant, I opened my eyes and instantly felt myself dive-bombing back to earth, gently landing on the couch beside Joe.

"What happened?" I asked, unable to mask my disappointment.

"You opened your eyes," Joe said, laughing. "It's one of the cardinal rules of flying in your dreams," he added. "I guess I should have warned you."

"But I wasn't really dreaming!" I protested. "I was wide awake with my eyes closed, is all."

"Semantics," he said.

"What does it mean, Joe?" I begged. "What is it about these poems that they showed up in my dreams last night and now they're right here in my lap, making me fly again? What's the lesson? I don't get it."

Wordlessly, Joe took the bundle of poems

from my reluctant hands, putting them aside on the coffee table with our now cold coffee and half-eaten bagels. He turned back to me then and clasped both of my hands inside his large, warm ones.

"All this time," he explained, "you've thought you were searching for a dream." His eyes explored mine, watching for any trace of resistance. "But the fact is, it is your dreams that have been searching for you."

"But . . ." I had a million questions and really no idea where to start.

"Shhh, shhh, shhh," Joe said, placing a finger over my lips and tucking the bundle of poems under his arm. He rose from the couch and headed for the front door, then turned soundlessly on his heel. "Trust me on this," he implored. "It's time to put you and your dreams in contact with each other. Once the wheels are set in motion like this, it doesn't take long at all. You'll see." Quietly, he let himself out.

I sat there for several stunned moments, and if it hadn't been for the phone beginning to ring, I don't know how long I would have stayed in that trance.

It was my personal trainer calling to see why I had missed that morning's appointment.

"Oh," I said, "I was busy painting."

*I*T WAS A WEEK BEFORE I was able to get another appointment with the personal trainer, and I could have sworn he was punishing me for the previous week's little oversight. The minute I showed up at the gym, he had me on my back doing stomach crunches, then pulling myself off the floor by climbing an "invisible rope." It was fifty minutes of pure torture, and I found myself wondering if a flawless body was really worth this much drudgery and suffering.

I tried to keep my mind off the pain by thinking about something pleasant, but the only idea that enticed me was the thought of a morphine injection. Then I remembered something Joe had said the other morning over coffee. It was something about how I put too much emphasis on having a perfect body because I hadn't realized what a perfect mind I have. For a brief moment I considered how much easier it might be to exercise my mind instead of my body, but then I don't imagine many people would pay to see my mind.

What had Joe meant by that? He specifically said it wasn't necessary for me to go to college, yet what could I possibly do with my *mind* that would pay for the lifestyle to which I was accustomed? I was obviously not the academic type, and I certainly was not a conformist. In fact, give me a set of rules and I feel compelled to break them. So how else could I possibly fit into this world except by doing exactly what I was doing? At least being a stripper paid the bills, and if stomach crunches had to be a part of it, then I guessed I'd just have to live with that.

The minute my torture session with the personal trainer was over, I headed for the Jacuzzi and the shower. The whole time though, I couldn't stop thinking about Joe and the things he had said. What had he meant about my dreams searching for me, and not the other way around? How had he known exactly where to find my poetry tied together with a blue ribbon, and how was that connected to the ability to fly in my dreams? I couldn't imagine that those flowery, tacky little poems of mine had any value, but why had he taken them with him? Most of all, why hadn't I heard from him in a week? Not that I'm the possessive type or anything like that, but the man had unbelievable charisma, and I wanted to see him again. Besides, he was teaching me things about myself that were fascinating.

Ever since Joe had breezed into my life, it seemed everything had changed. I felt like a tulip bulb that someone had planted long ago, then neglected. All along, I had thought it was God who had forgotten me, but now I was learning that I was the responsible party. I was the one who had been treating myself so shabbily.

Nowadays, I could actually feel Joe's warmth and presence shining down on me, and I was filled with an overwhelming urge to grow and to burst through the surface of things that were holding me back. It was as though a magical mist of well-being had settled over me, allowing me to see life more clearly than I had ever thought possible. I found myself filled with a sense of hope lately and was pleasantly surprised at the domino effect it was having on me. For one thing, I was no longer obsessed with sizing up the financial potential of my clients, but had begun instead, to consider my own dormant and untapped possibilities.

I knew I had to be careful though. It was incredibly easy to become very attached to Joe, and I knew that wouldn't be a good idea. After all, he had told me again just last week that his time with me was limited. Sooner or later, simply by definition of his mission, he would have to move on to the next person who needed his help. In my line of work, staying detached from people is a requirement, so you wouldn't think I'd have any trouble keeping my emotional balance in this situation. Usually it's very easy for me to keep my distance, but Joe was putting me in touch with all kinds of feelings lately, and I was finding it impossible not to fall in love with him a little more each day.

I realized I was going to have to try harder not to let my guard down.

I slung my gym bag over my shoulder and made my way out to the parking lot. Refusing to let myself obsess about Joe anymore and why he hadn't called, I punched the radio on as soon as I started the engine and began flipping around for a good station. I felt like singing.

I was sitting at a red light on Wilshire Boulevard when I hit upon my all-time favorite song, "Someone to Watch Over Me." Absently, I sang along as I waited for the light to change.

The first few cars in the opposite direction had their left-turn signals on, and I marveled at their ambition. This was a particularly busy intersection, even by LA standards, and even the most aggressive drivers often end up sitting through that light a few times before getting the chance to make that left turn. Grateful that I just had to go straight across, I turned up the radio and sang louder. Being the closet-poet that I am, I changed the title to "Someone to Make Over Me" and I made up my own lyrics as I went along.

There's a certain man who makes me
   feel free,
Fills me with glee,
Then patiently
Begins to make over me.

The light turned green then, but the woman in the car in front of me just sat there waving to the cars across the intersection to go ahead and make their turn. Being as this is LA, nobody over there trusted that this woman would really forfeit her right-of-way and let them go, so no one moved at all. Cars behind me started honking their horns in frustration, but still the car ahead of me didn't move.

Inevitably, the light turned red again, and not one of us had made it through the intersection.

I took a deep breath for a big finish and sang even louder now to quell my frustration.

Won't you tell him now that my love is
 real,
Now I can feel
A brand-new zeal
Each time he makes over meeeee.

Just as I was holding that last note, I heard someone applauding from the passenger seat. Startled, my eyes flew open to find Joe sitting beside me, smirking boyishly and clapping those graceful hands together in approval.

"Is there no such thing as privacy with *you* around?!" I blurted out, more embarrassed than startled. "Is nothing sacred?" I wondered why it was so hard for me to stop being defensive and sarcastic even when I loved someone.

"Everything is sacred," he said, grinning, "especially moments like this, when you are totally unself-conscious and just enjoying yourself. And as for the sarcastic attitude, well, that's just part of your charm. You'll mellow sooner or later anyway. Besides," he added, "I thought you were singing about *me.* Weren't you?"

"Don't flatter yourself," I lamely replied, knowing that of course he knew the truth, which was that I was crazy about him.

The light turned green again, and this time the car in front of me moved without hesitation across the intersection and traffic flowed smoothly again. Well, as smoothly as it can move in LA.

"Good, I'm glad she finally caught on," Joe said, looking up ahead to the woman who had caused the traffic snarl. "I'll have to make a note of that."

"Don't tell me you even keep track of traffic violations," I said accusingly.

He shook his head and laughed. "Is that what you think?" he asked, raising an eyebrow in surprise. "That I'm keeping score of her mistakes so I can punish her for them? Really, Heather, when are you ever going to trust me?'' His tone was kind and ever patient, and for a fleeting moment, I wondered how he put up with me, with any of us.

"Well, I would have thought you'd approve of her behavior anyway,'' I said stubbornly. "I mean she was being passive and yielding, just the way I thought you liked people to be. Especially women,'' I couldn't help but add.

"She had the right-of-way,'' he said simply.

"So?'' I responded, getting sarcastic again. "She gave it up for the sake of other people. I would think you'd give her a big fat gold star for that.''

"Her behavior didn't serve her highest purpose,'' he explained matter-of-factly. "All it did was mess up the flow of things.''

I didn't quite know what to say to that. For once, I had no cynical comeback, just a strong suspicion that Joe was using this rather minor example to teach me an even bigger concept.

"You see, Heather,'' he continued, "there's nothing wrong with accepting what is rightfully yours. It keeps things moving in the right direction. It's when you do this self-flagellating thing—you know, thinking you're not good enough or that you don't deserve good things—that you not only hurt yourself, but you impair everyone around you as well."

It took me several minutes to digest that one. "Wow," I finally said. "You're nothing like the nuns said you were."

He laughed at that and agreed, "Yeah, I've got my work cut out with that group."

We drove for several more minutes in silence then, and I was thinking what a great guy he was. So understanding. So forgiving and compassionate. And with a sense of humor too. I felt incredibly close to him at that moment in spite of myself, closer to a man than I had ever before allowed myself to get.

"This is just the beginning," he said softly, in response to my thoughts. "Life for you, Heather Hurley, is just going to keep getting better and better now."

"Can I take that to the bank?" I asked, not even daring to hope that he was serious.

"You'll see," he said with absolute certainty. "It's your turn now. You're about to discover the meaning of fulfillment and contentment."

I was surprised at the tears that immediately sprang to my eyes when he said that. Feelings of relief and hope and joy washed over me like a refreshing ocean wave, and though it was a lovely feeling, it was completely foreign to me. I wondered why the thought of being happy suddenly made me want to cry. What was wrong with me?

"Don't be concerned," he said knowingly. "Even happiness takes some getting used to. Especially when you've been deprived of it for a long time. You'll adjust."

"I will?" I asked, relieved that he understood so completely what I was feeling. It was the very first time in my life that I felt someone actually understood me and a giant tear rolled down my cheek and slid off my chin. Embarrassed by my tears, I forced a laugh and asked, "Do you think you could insult me or slap me around or something? *That* I definitely know how to handle. But this happiness stuff seems awfully complicated. I don't know what to do with it."

Ever so tenderly, Joe reached over and

wiped another one of my tears with the back of his hand. "When you drive, you should drive," he said, "and when you cry, you should cry. The two don't mix real well. Why don't you pull into that parking lot right over there?"

"I'm okay," I protested, uncomfortable with the possibility of giving myself permission to really let my tears out. I suppose I was afraid that if I ever started, I might never stop.

"You're far more than just okay," he said sweetly, "but why don't you pull over anyway?"

183

I did as he said and pulled into the parking lot of a little shopping center. I thought it odd that I had driven down this street at least a thousand times before, but the presence of this little mall had escaped my notice. I wondered why.

Joe produced an immaculate white handkerchief and wiped the tears from my face. "That's it," he encouraged lovingly as I wept, "get it all out."

And I did. I cried for my lost childhood and

for the defensive behaviors I'd adopted to keep people from getting too close to me. I cried for the missed opportunities of really loving another human being, and I cried for the many years that I had not even been able to love myself. The broken dreams, the lack of self-esteem, the fear of the future, all of it somehow poured from my heart and out through my eyes, and Joe caught every pain-filled teardrop in his handkerchief.

"That's very good, Heather," he comforted. "You're almost done now."

"Done with what?" I sniffled, too engrossed in my emotions to put on any airs.

"Grieving over the past," he answered knowingly. "You can't make room for the good things in your life till you let go of the past." He watched me cry a moment longer, then added, "And there's a lot of that good stuff just waiting to catch up with you. I promise."

I looked at him blankly, then took the handkerchief from his hands and blew my nose.

When finally I had pulled myself together and stopped crying, I began hiccuping. Joe looked at me lovingly and noted, "Have you any idea how adorable you are when you hiccup?"

At first I laughed; then I threw my arms around him and laid my aching head on his warm, strong shoulder, trying to etch this feeling of peace and utter safety into my memory forever. We had shared so much of ourselves, and I loved him so completely. He sat there quietly, stroking my hair and soothing me like a parent soothes a frightened child.

Then I remembered something. For some reason I got a flashback of Dorothy in *The Wizard of Oz*. I remembered how she, the scarecrow, the lion, and the tin man all approached the wizard and how he had pulled something out of his black bag for each of her three friends. When they asked what was in the bag for Dorothy, I remembered her saying something like, "Oh, I don't think there's anything in that big black bag for me."

Joe's hand slid from my hair to my shoulder at that moment, and he whispered in my ear, "Why are you thinking about Dorothy and the Wizard of Oz?"

"Because I feel a little like Dorothy right now," I said between hiccups. "Everyone else seems to get their prize in life, but I don't think there's anything left in that big black bag for me. I'm here on my own, just drifting around till something happens. I wish I could be like everyone else, but I know I'll never fit in. I've always marched to the beat of a different drum. That's just how I am. Different."

I thought I heard Joe laugh at that, and I was a bit offended that he would take my innermost feelings so lightly.

He pulled me away from the shelter of his shoulder and turned me to face him. "I'm not laughing at your feelings, Heather," he said sincerely. "I'm laughing at the foolishness of your fears. First of all, I think you know by now that you are never alone or unloved, but in case you need to hear it, here it is. I love you, Heather Hurley, and I will always be with you, even when you're unable to perceive me with your five physical senses."

I could feel my heart actually melting as the love in his eyes gave indisputable meaning to his words.

"And as for marching to the beat of a different drum," he continued, "well, at least you hear the beat. Have you any idea how many people go through life completely deaf to the rhythms of their own inner desires and dreams?"

187

I was beginning to feel better suddenly, and a feeling of overwhelming love engulfed me. At least, I assumed it was love. It was hard to tell because I had nothing to compare it to.

"And as far as that mysterious black bag is concerned," he was saying, "it's far from empty. I don't have any magical badges of love or courage or intelligence to pin on you, Heather, only a heart full of love. And love is the only magic you will ever need. It's the answer to everything. But it all begins with *self*-love. Remember that."

I didn't know what to say. Here I was, sitting

in my car in some unfamiliar parking lot, discovering the path to hope and joy. Nothing in my outer world had changed, but somehow I was certain that my inner world was undergoing some major reconstruction. I couldn't wait to lift the drop cloths someday and see the end result.

Joe was smiling when I looked up at him again. "C'mon," he said, letting himself out of the car. "I have something to show you."

I would have followed him anywhere at that point, but he led me into a charming little card store on the edge of the mall. A bell tinkled over our heads as we stepped across the flowery welcome mat, and the scent of sandalwood and vanilla tinged the air.

A stylishly dressed, fiftyish woman appeared from a back room and smiled warmly at us. Then she did a double take when she looked at Joe.

"Joe," she breathed, unable to disguise the delight in her voice. "Is it really you?"

"It's really me, Stella," he said, approaching the counter and embracing her fondly for a moment. "I told you I was going to keep tabs on you." Then turning toward me, he added, "This is my friend, Heather Hurley."

The woman looked a little surprised but covered it quickly with her good manners. *"The* Heather Hurley?" she asked almost reverently. "Heather Hurley of 'The Dream Collection'?" she added with a warm smile directed at me.

"The one and only," Joe answered. "Mind if I show her around?"

189

The woman nodded knowingly, and for some strange reason, I became fixated on the tinkling of the gold charm bracelet she wore on her slender left wrist. The Dream Collection? What did they mean by that? How did this woman know me? I had no idea what was going on, but Joe took me by the hand and led me to a display in the front of the store.

There, amid costly looking novelty items and potpourri, was a display of greeting cards with a sign over them that read, "The Dream Collection, by Heather Hurley." Mesmerized by what I saw, I delicately picked up a card from the rack and studied it with all the wonder of a mother gazing at her newborn baby.

"Your kisses engulf me like a flock of butterflies," it read. I picked up another one and it said, "I thought it was the sun that warmed me so gently; then I opened my eyes and realized it was your love." I scanned several more cards, and each had sentiments on them that I remembered writing years ago, when I was yearning for romance. When I still believed in love.

How had they ended up here? I had packed up my hopes and dreams and poetry long ago, tied them together with a blue ribbon, and tucked them in the bottom of my hope chest. How could this have happened? Bewildered, I turned to Joe . . . and then I remembered.

"I hope you don't mind," he said, eyes shining with pride. "I talked to a friend of mine who happens to own a greeting card business, and I showed him your work. He fell in love with it. Says there's a real market for this kind of thing. So he bought the line, for a very nice price, I might add, and put one of his graphic artists on it right away to design the covers. What do you think?"

"B-but how did it all happen so fast? That sounds i-impossible," I stammered.

"Nothing's impossible, Heather. I thought you knew that by now," he said, placing a loving hand on my shoulder. "Besides, I told you that once the wheels of your dreams are set in motion, it doesn't take any time at all to make them a reality. Remember?"

I was flabbergasted. I heard every word, but my mind had a hard time registering what he was saying. I thought maybe I was going to faint, because all of a sudden I lost my peripheral vision, but I sensed Joe's presence emanating some kind of power that miraculously kept me on my feet. I heard no sound either, except for the odd tinkling of Stella's charm bracelet again.

Carefully, Joe pulled an envelope from the inside pocket of his ever-present motorcycle jacket and handed it to me. "It's a check from my friend, the greeting card guy. He says you'll get royalties too, depending on how well they sell."

"They've been selling like hotcakes," Stella added from behind the counter. "I can't keep them in stock." Then she added kindly, "I do hope you'll keep writing more of them, Heather. Most people can't express their feelings as beautifully as you can."

I stared at Stella, then back at Joe. I was dumbfounded. How could this be happening? Me? Heather Hurley doing something that took real talent—talent that came from my *mind?* Filling a gap in other people's lives?

"Why is that so surprising?" Joe asked. "You have a myriad of talents. You just need to believe in yourself."

"I don't know how to do that," I answered honestly. "I haven't had much practice."

Joe and Stella exchanged understanding smiles.

"Maybe this is a good time to begin," Stella offered quietly. She came out from behind the counter then and stood beside us. Plucking one of the cards from The Dream Collection, she held it up with perfectly manicured, tapered fingers and gazed at it fondly. "You obviously have a gift for putting feelings into words. The proof, if you even need proof, is that people are happy to pay for the way you express what's on their minds. How could you *not* believe in yourself?"

"But I wrote that stuff a long time ago," I protested, again strangely hypnotized by the little charm bracelet on her wrist. "I don't know if I still have it in me."

"You still have it in you." Joe smiled. "I gave you that talent for a reason, so there is no doubt that you can still do it. Besides, I told my friend you'd have a new slew of them within the next thirty days, so you'd better *start* believing in yourself."

It was then that I realized why I was so drawn to Stella's charm bracelet. My mouth dropped open as I noticed that each charm had something written on it, something that looked suspiciously like her own set of personal commandments.

Without asking permission, I reached for her wrist and held up one of the charms to read the inscription on it.

"We are all teachers. Teach others what is in the magic black bag of life for them."

Stunned, I looked from Stella's sparkling blue eyes to Joe's warm brown ones, and I have never in my life felt such love or energy . . . or belief in myself.

"You see, Dorothy," Joe said with a twinkle in his eye, "that big, black bag wasn't empty after all."

Epilogue

RIVING TO THE CLUB
that night, I felt light-headed with relief. I
had made a decision of monumental propor-
tions, and I intended to stick to it. I had
decided to never again work at a job that did
not bring me joy, and driving to the club now
to pick up my costumes and to inform Anthony of my resignation was the first step in
keeping that promise to myself.

I was surprised at the magnitude of utter
freedom I was feeling as I put the top down on

my little BMW and let the wind blow through my hair, for once not caring how I'd look when I arrived. I basked in that glorious feeling all the way up the 405 freeway, realizing that I must have been feeling more trapped than I had been willing to admit.

But no more.

I was going to start a new life. I wasn't sure how much money I could make on my own greeting-card line; I only knew I had to try. "Painting pictures with words" was something I had always loved to do, and thanks to Joe, now I saw a way of supporting myself by doing what I loved. Besides, I had a nice little nest egg already socked away in my "life-after-forty fund" that I was willing to tap into if necessary. I also had the surprisingly generous check Joe's friend had written me for the poems.

The fact is, I had almost fallen off my chair when I got home and saw the amount Joe's friend had been willing to pay for something that I had thought had no value. How Joe had worked out the legalities of the contract and such, I have no idea. All I know is, it's not always a smart thing to question the universe when you suddenly find yourself in flow with it. I didn't want to be like that lady in the traffic jam that morning who had forfeited her right-of-way. You don't have to hit *me* over the head with a brick.

I pulled into the darkened parking lot and didn't even bother to lock up the car, since I didn't plan to be more than a few minutes. I took a deep breath and, just for a moment, wallowed in the immensely satisfying knowledge that I would never again use my body as just another form of currency.

Heading toward the stairs and the backstage door, I noticed the dark shape of a motorcycle, a Harley-Davidson in fact, in the far corner of the parking lot. I knew that none of the guys who worked here as bouncers rode a Harley. Anthony, of course, had always wanted to, but he was definitely *not* the Harley type. Not in his wildest dreams.

Then it hit me. Joe was here. I suppose he thought I might need some moral support, and I laughed at the pun as I pulled open the heavy back door.

The place was empty and quiet except for the distant voices of the hired help preparing for tonight's show. I headed directly for my dressing station and started emptying drawers into the plastic bags I'd brought. Then, grabbing an armload of my costumes on the way out, I made my way to the car and dumped my stash into the backseat. That left only one more task. I had to go back inside one last time to find that little worm Anthony and tell him he'd seen the last of me.

Reluctantly, I began climbing the back stairs; then something struck me and I stopped in my tracks. Why was I always walking through the back doors of life? Didn't I deserve to walk through front doors like everyone else? I realized that I never wanted to walk through a back door again. With that, I squared my shoulders, descended the stairs, and walked around the side of the building . . . toward the front entrance.

It's funny how something as seemingly insignificant as which door you walk through can have an effect on you, but believe me, it does. I swear I felt an awesome sense of empowerment simply by refusing to go through that rear entrance even one more time and heading for the front door instead.

The piano player must have been practicing for tonight's opening number, because I could hear the tinkling notes wafting out into the warm, summer evening. I'd been hearing that same music for a lot of years now, but for once, it actually sounded pretty to me. Maybe it had something to do with hearing it from the front door instead of the back door. I listened for a moment from outside; then, head held high, I opened the door and let myself in.

It was odd to see the club from this angle for a change. What had always been routine and hideously boring to me was suddenly rather enticing when I looked at it through the eyes of the customers. I scanned the room for Anthony, but there was no trace of him. Come to think of it, I didn't see Joe anywhere either, though I was certain that was his Harley parked out back.

The only people in the room, other than the piano player and the bartender, were a handful of some of our regulars, sitting at the bar getting a head start on the evening. I recognized each and every one of them, though I didn't know one of them by name.

The burly looking guy on the end had once paid me two hundred dollars to dance on his table with my back to him. The guy in the middle had once waited outside for me and tried to convince me that one date with him would turn my life around. The conservative-looking guy on the far end of the bar was the one I had noticed the other night. He had only recently started coming in, and he had an almost tragic look about him. He always sat by himself, quietly getting drunk, but never became rude or disorderly. Though he drank like a fish, his body was strong and well toned, suggesting that his self-destructive alcohol habit was a fairly new one. I can always tell a seasoned drunk, and this guy was definitely a novice.

I walked up to the bar and nodded to Jimmy, the bartender. I don't think he recognized me at first, since he's only seen me on the other side of the stage, wearing spike heels and seductive little costumes, a far cry from the T-shirt, shorts, and sneakers I was wearing tonight.

"You seen Anthony?" I asked, ignoring his shocked look.

"Yeah, he's in his office with some agent. He should be out in a minute," Jimmy said, still studying my "normal person" ensemble.

"An agent?" I asked, a little surprised myself now. "What, like a DEA- or FBI-type person?"

Jimmy shook his head and smiled as he slid another Jack Daniel's toward the novice drunk on the end. "Nah," he said, "a talent agent or something."

"A talent agent? What would a talent agent be doing in a dump like this?" I said, thinking that I shouldn't be saying something like that in front of the customers. Then I realized it didn't matter what I said anymore. Once I got through the uncomfortable ordeal of telling Anthony I quit, I'd never have to see this place again. With new confidence, I added, "Who in this place could possibly think they're talented enough to warrant an agent?"

"You tell me," Jimmy said. "He says he's representing you."

"Me?" I scoffed. "That's a laugh. No way do I have an agent!"

No sooner had the words fallen out of my mouth, than the office door opened and out walked Anthony, shaking hands with Joe. They both looked in my direction then and seemed genuinely glad to see me.

"Your agent's a great guy, Heather," Antho-
ny spouted before I could ask what the heck Joe thought he was doing. "I didn't know you had such good taste. Good luck with the audition, hear?"

The audition? What was he talking about? I wanted to deluge them both with questions, but Anthony and Joe were shaking hands again. Anthony slapped Joe on the back one last time then and disappeared into the back room. The next thing I knew, a very handsome and well-dressed man came through the front door and waved to Joe.

"Fred," Joe said, smiling, "I'll be with you in a minute. Make yourself at home."

Joe turned to me then, a broad grin playing across those curvy lips.

"What's going on around here?" I demanded. "Has everyone lost their marbles?"

"It must seem that way to you." Joe laughed. "Fred over there just opened a very posh, very swanky cocktail lounge in Beverly Hills," he explained, "and he's looking for a very special kind of torch singer. You know, someone with class to add a little ambience."

"So what has that got to do with me?" I insisted. "I'm afraid to ask," I added, already suspecting the answer.

"Well, you always wanted to be a lounge singer," Joe answered, unable to hide the amusement in his voice. "I mean, it's not exactly Vegas, but it's a start."

I was very confused now. Was I supposed to audition right here and now? With no material? No preparation? And why had Joe arranged this anyway? Didn't he think I could make it in the greeting-card business? Had he suddenly changed his mind about that?

Not surprisingly, he heard my thoughts and read the apprehensive look on my face. He slid a reassuring arm around my shoulders and squeezed me close to him for a moment. "Heather, relax," he said, smiling. "Your greeting-card line is going to be very successful. It's a done deal as far as the universe is concerned. I just thought maybe you could use this singing gig to put some fun and balance into your life, not to mention some extra cash. You know, just to make sure you don't get bored or obsessed with any one thing."

"Variety is the spice of life, is that what you're saying?" I surmised.

"Something like that," he agreed. "But the concept of balance is the key here. You don't ever want to do any one thing to excess," he explained, "because if you do, even something you love can turn into something you resent after a while."

I was overwhelmed once again by the number of profound concepts Joe constantly spouted. "How am I ever going to remember all these smart things you say?" I asked, afraid to trust them only to my memory.

"Funny you should ask," Joe answered,

reaching for a gift-wrapped box on top of the piano and handing it to me. "You know our time together is just about up," he murmured.

"What?" I gasped. "Oh, Joe, no. Oh, please, no." Tears immediately stung my eyes, and I watched two of them plunk onto the gift-wrapped box in my hand.

"Go ahead and open it, Heather," he said softly. "It will help you understand."

I did as he said and numbly opened the package. Inside was a box of cream-colored stationery with a celestial design of birds flying through the heavens. Alongside the stationery was an exquisite gold pen with a feather on it. I didn't know what to say.

"Read what it says," he gently instructed.

I removed the cover that bound the pages and recognized a list of personal commandments, *my* commandments, printed on the top of every page:

1. *Pain and panic are your friends, trying to show you a better way.*
2. *Look only for the good in people and that's exactly what you'll find.*

3. *Let go of the past to make room for the future.*
4. *History is not irreversible.*
5. *Graciously embrace what is rightfully yours.*
6. *Balance is the key to a fulfilled life.*
7. *Believe in your many talents.*

I looked up at Joe just as another tear slid down my face. I shook my head. "No, Joe. You can't leave," I pleaded. "I'm not ready for that yet."

"Yes, you are," he assured me. "You just don't know it. You really need to work on believing in yourself, okay?"

"Okay," I sniffled. "But I'm sure gonna miss you."

He took the feathered pen from my hand then and held it up. "This isn't just any pen." He smiled. "It came from that magic black bag. Anytime you want to talk to me, write your thoughts and concerns on paper with this pen. Then write what you think my answer to you would be, and I promise you, I will speak to you through this pen. It will be me guiding your hand. Don't ever doubt that, Heather."

Goose bumps ran up and down my spine when he said that, and it didn't escape his notice. He glanced upward for a split second, and his smile widened. Then he looked directly into my eyes and held me spellbound with his love. "Goose bumps are an exclamation point from the universe," he explained. "Whenever you get them, try to remember that something important or even cosmic has just happened."

Glancing down at the stationery, I suddenly remembered something. "Joe, what about my flying dream?" I asked. "Did it mean that my poems, you know, my greeting-card business, will give me wings to fly?"

"Very good," he said proudly.

"But what about the kiss on the paper? What did that mean?" I asked, trying to cram all of my questions in before he left.

"That I love you, of course."

Joe loved me. It was all so simple and so beautiful. At that moment I knew there weren't any more important questions.

Reading my thoughts again and smiling with satisfaction, Joe murmured, "This might be a good time to start the audition."

I wasn't even nervous. I had no music, no preparation, and no idea even what song to sing, but what I did know now was that Joe would never let me down. That always there was a gift wrapped inside everything that occurred in my life. I may not always recognize the gift, but inevitably, it would eventually become clear to me.

"Why don't you sing that little number you did so well in the car this morning?" Joe suggested. "You know, the one with the lyrics you made up."

With that, he kissed the top of my head and sauntered toward the bar, taking a seat next to the novice alcoholic. I suppose he wanted to watch me from a distance. A distance that I knew would grow longer and longer until, eventually, my only contact with him would be through my written words.

Tinkling notes from the piano floated past my ears then, and I turned toward "Fred," giving him one of the first genuine smiles I'd felt in a long time. I reached for the microphone and at the same time, reached into some unexplored place inside me to find the voice of passion that I knew had always been there, just waiting to be discovered.

I knew this would be the last time I would see Joe in this lifetime and that these lyrics might be the last words I would ever speak directly to him. Corny as it may sound, I wanted to dedicate the song to him. I wanted to prove somehow that he had changed my life and that I had learned my lessons well. It was important for me to give something of an introduction at this point that would show him just how much I had learned and how important he would always be to me.

I spoke softly and lovingly into the microphone, holding back tears that wanted more than anything to be brushed away by his gentle hands, just one more time.

"This one's for all of us who aren't going to walk through back doors anymore," I announced, as the piano player gave me my cue and I began to sing a spur-of-the-moment, homemade introduction:

> *There's a man I know, says that I'm*
> > *misled;*
> *Still I must insist, that's how I was bred.*
> *But I'm going to let him try*
> *To tell me why.*

The music picked up, and though I couldn't see very well past the light in my eyes, I sensed Joe's warm and approving smile. I watched his silhouette as he struck up a conversation with the novice alcoholic beside him, and suddenly I knew who was next on his list. It didn't matter though because somehow I knew that Joe would always be listening to me.

> *Looking everywhere just to find his*
> > *love—*
> *He's the greatest friend I've been*
> > *dreamin' of,*
> *Only man I trust with all my heart.*

I didn't recognize my own voice for the smooth silkiness of it. The words flowed easily from some creative center in my brain, and the feelings that welled up within me fanned the love that smoldered in my heart. For once, I understood the power of art and creativity and the immense satisfaction of unleashing your unique talents into the world. The best part was that I didn't expect or necessarily want anything in return.

I noticed a few more customers had begun to straggle in, and they stood quietly in the doorway as I sang. If any of them recognized me as Heather Harley, the stripper, they kept it to themselves.

I belted out a few more lines, then prepared for a big finish as I directed my gaze to where Joe had been sitting. Not surprisingly, his chair was empty now and so was the one next to him, but I knew exactly where he was and what he was doing. He was on his Harley no doubt, somehow rescuing one more lost soul in the world, probably the one who'd been sitting next to him at the bar. I heard the distant roar of his Harley's engine from the back parking lot, and I felt goose bumps again. The universe had sent me another exclamation point, and I used my joy to belt out the next few lines over the thunder of his takeoff.

> *Although he may be the man some folks*
> *think of as distant,*
> *In my world, he showed me the way.*
> *Won't you tell him now that my love is*
> *real?*
> *Now I can feel*
> *A brand-new zeal*
> *Each time he makes over me.*

A few of the patrons began applauding; then their applause spread like a California wildfire. I smiled and nodded my thanks to them as I put down the microphone and walked over to Fred.

"You're hired," was all he said. And I noticed goose bumps on his arms too.